MARKED FOR STRIFE

SUSAN HAYES

Copyright © 2022 Susan Hayes

Marked For Strife (Book two of the Crashed and Claimed series)

First print Publication: May 2022

Editor: Amanda Brown

Cover Art: Croco Designs

Published by: Black Scroll Publications Ltd

ABOUT THE BOOK

**It was supposed to be the trip of a lifetime…
now she's just trying to stay alive.**

Rissa can't believe her luck. She won an all-expenses-paid trip on a luxury matchmaking cruise. She's not looking for love, but a few weeks of five-star pampering while seeing the galaxy sounds perfect… until it all goes wrong.

Abandoning ship isn't on her itinerary and neither is the growly but oh-so-sexy alien who is half convinced she's the enemy and utterly certain she's *his*. She's got a list of the reasons they're wrong for each other, but when they're together, everything just feels right.

Crash landing on a prison planet may not be the vacation she dreamed of, but it might turn out to be the best "worst" day of her life.

***Buckle up. This sci-fi romance contains an alien with fur, fangs, horns, and a very possessive attitude when it comes to the woman he's claimed for his own.*

1

———

RISSA CHECKED the timer and grunted. She still had ten minutes to go, fifteen if she was serious about burning off that extra slice of cake she'd indulged in before bed. The food on this cruise was the best she'd ever had, and it was worth every extra minute of sweat to enjoy it while she could. In a few more weeks she'd be back to her normal life, where food, water, and even air were carefully rationed commodities.

Life on a space station wasn't easy, but it was the only life she'd ever known. If her number hadn't come up in the annual lottery, she might have spent her entire life on Nanu station. She'd have missed out on discovering the glorious indulgences of spending an entire day at a spa, eating every meal from an endless buffet, and sleeping in a bed the size of a standard living cubby back home.

She also would have gone her whole life not knowing how mind-twistingly terrifying planets were. Not the planets themselves but all the things that came with them—toxic plants, dangerous animals, the inescapable pull of gravity, and worst of all, open sky. Just the thought of it made her miss her footing and nearly stumble off the treadmill.

"That's it. I'm done for the day." She kept hold of the rail with one hand as she slowed the machine down to a gentle walk. At least no one was around to see her nearly fall on her face. A few weeks ago, it would have been thronging with fit, trim women obsessed about every ounce of body fat and running on the treadmills as if all the demons of hell were chasing them with ice cream sundaes and extra fudge sauce... and now she wanted ice cream slathered in ribbons of warm, gooey chocolate and caramel.

She still had dessert on the brain when it all went to the hells in nine hypersonic handcarts. The deck beneath her feet shuddered, the hull creaking in ways that set Rissa's teeth on edge. It was the sound of a ship in pain. She'd heard it plenty of times before, but that had been at the shipyard where she worked, surrounded by teams of professionals with everything they needed to put things right.

They weren't anywhere near her shipyard right now. They were in open space, not the ideal location for their hyperdrive to fail... But that's what was happening.

"Shit!" Training had her running for the engineering deck before she could think. It was instinctive, and she made it out the door of the gym and into the corridor before she remembered she wasn't on duty. She wasn't even a crewmember. She was a passenger, and she didn't even have access to that part of the ship. She stopped running, automatically moving to press against the wall so she wasn't blocking the corridor. With the drive down, they'd have dropped into normal space. That wasn't a problem so long as they weren't too close to a planet or a star.

Klaxons erupted, the noise almost drowning out the captain's orders as she spoke over the ship-wide comms.

Rissa decoded the various alarms. Navigation and proximity alerts screamed as engine failure alarms wailed. Airtight doors slammed shut and locked. That shouldn't happen. Not unless they were... *Fuck.*

The gym and other amenities were one deck below the passenger quarters, meaning the escape pods were in a different spot. She'd spent years working on ships like these. Hells, she'd even worked on this particular vessel, and she knew exactly where to go. The only other passenger she ran across was dressed in a spa robe and slippers, and she clearly didn't have a clue what to do.

Rissa grabbed the younger woman by the arm and hustled her down the corridor. "This way," she yelled so her words would carry over the alarms.

Hope shot her look of gratitude mixed in with a healthy dollop of fear. "What's happening?" she called back.

The deck bucked beneath them, hard enough to make both of them stumble, but their hold on each other kept them on their feet.

"Bad shit. Maybe an attack." It was impossible to convey much information over the noise, and they needed to move, not talk.

Hope's eyes widened. "Attack?"

All Rissa's worst fears were confirmed a second later. Another alarm wailed, drowning out all the others. The main lights winked out and were replaced by red strobe lights. *Shit.* It was time to go. The order to abandon ship had gone out.

"Come on! We need to go. Now!" Rissa knew they were running out of time. The ship was under massive stress, and she felt it twist and ripple beneath her feet. It was damaged, crippled, and fighting against a significant source of gravity... and it was losing.

They reached the evac station. The pod doors were all open and waiting. She pushed Hope to the nearest one.

"Sit down and put the harness on. That's all you need to do. The rest is automatic. Just hang on, be smart, and don't go too far from your pod."

Hope gave her a tight, quick nod and ducked inside.

Rissa waited for three long seconds before moving to the next pod in the row. The first pod sealed before she got inside her own. Hope was as safe as Rissa could make her. The rest was up to her.

Once her own pod dropped free of the ship, Rissa got busy. No way would she sit back and let this thing pilot itself. That was fine for someone with no flight training, but she'd been fixing ships most of her life. That meant she knew how to fly them... more or less. Either way, this pod would crash. That's what they were designed for. Her plan was to make sure it crashed as gently as possible.

"And this is why I prefer to fly myself." Rissa looked around the clearing she'd chosen as her landing site. She and the pod were both in one piece, and the only damage she'd done to the area was a few scorch marks on the grass-covered ground.

She'd maintained the same trajectory the autopilot had determined. She didn't want to wind up too far away from any other survivors. When rescue came, proximity might make the difference between going home and getting stuck here for the rest of her life. That was *not* going to happen.

It could turn out to be the nicest planet in existence, but it was still a planet. That meant weather, and animals, and an atmosphere that was only held in place by gravity. No domes, no containment units, and no barriers.

"It's not natural," she grumbled. "At least, not to me." She didn't do nature. The closest she'd come to it was the bio-dome at the heart of Nanu station, but that small area of carefully cultured trees and plants had about as much in common with this place as a candle flame had to a solar flare.

The clearing was covered in some kind of knee-high plant she thought might be called grass. A current of air moved the long blades of orange and gold, making them hiss and rustle. The sound made her uneasy, though she didn't know why.

She kept her eyes on the ground with most of her focus on her feet. That way she couldn't see the sky at all, which helped... a little. She needed to retrieve the emergency supplies stored in the pod and drag them over to the tree line. Under the trees, everything was in shadow, and that meant she'd have another layer between her and the open air.

The trees were strange and nothing like the ones she'd seen in the biosphere. They were the wrong color for one thing. Those trees had been green and blue, but these were very different. Reds and oranges mostly, with a few flashes of golden yellow. The trunks were massive things, gnarled and twisted into thick towers that rose far into the air.

She caught herself looking up, squawked in horror, and dropped her eyes back to the ground again. Vertigo hit, and the next thing she knew, she was on her hands and knees as the world spun around her. She squeezed her eyes shut and dug her fingers into the grass as if that was the only thing stopping her from flying off into space.

When the spinning stopped, she didn't open her eyes right away. She just stayed where she was and tried not to throw up. "I fucking *hate* planets," she groaned as she waited for the queasiness to subside. Once it had, she hauled herself to her feet and made her way back to the pod. She had shit to do, and the faster she got it done, the sooner she'd be inside her emergency shelter. She needed a roof over her head as quickly as possible.

She dragged everything over to the edge of the clearing and arranged the carton with the emergency shelter so the entrance pointed toward the forest. She followed the instructions printed on the side, doing a sweep to make sure the area was clear of rocks and other debris that might puncture the shelter once she activated it. Then she leaned down and pressed the large button below the instructions. First she heard an explosive whoosh followed by a loud, prolonged hiss of air, and then the shelter inflated. It expanded away from her position, just the way it was supposed to.

Once that was done, she lugged a second container inside, sealed the doorway, and sat down on the floor with a sigh of relief. Yellow had never been her favorite color, but right now the garish Day-Glo shelter was the most beautiful sight she'd ever seen. Now she just had to make herself as comfortable as possible and wait for rescue. Surely that wouldn't take long. Humans weren't signatories to the Galactic Legion's Unified Agreement, but they were recognized as sentient lifeforms. Anyone who heard the *Bountiful Harvest's* distress beacon would be compelled to offer assistance. It was legion law.

That meant someone would come for them. In fact, they were probably already on their way.

2

THE STRIDENT CHIRP of electronics shattered the quiet and sent Strife rushing through the branches down to the deck of Mayhem's home. The alarm could only mean one thing: They were under attack.

He let gravity speed him on his way, and within seconds, he landed a few paces behind his clanmates. They were already at the small hut that housed the tracking equipment, which acted as an early warning system. Strife joined them, elbowing Menace until the massive male moved over enough that Strife could see into the dim interior.

"We're about to have company," Mayhem announced.

Menace snarled, the sound as dangerous as the male's chosen name.

No more work would be done today. Mayhem's new roof would have to wait until after the hunt. The verexi had sent more mercenaries to try and kill them, and some of his brothers had bets going on how many times their former captors would try before they gave up. Strife didn't think the scrawnies ever would. Not until all proof of their misdeeds and miscalculations were wiped from existence.

The screen inside the hut showed multiple vessels had breached the planet's atmosphere. He counted at least three small ships with several more blurs that could be threats or might be nothing more than static. Their tech was all salvage, and most of it was repurposed into whatever they needed it to be. He should know. He'd built most of it.

The three small ships were descending fast, and none of them would land in the same place. One looked like it would come down in Menace's territory, another in Mayhem's, and the last one would set down well inside the area he'd claimed for himself. Fools. They were making it easy to hunt them down.

The large ship was on a different course entirely. It was headed for the far side of a range of hills that lay beyond their established territory. He pointed to the screen. "Why land their main force there?" he asked. What possible tactical advantage did it give them to scatter their forces so widely?

Mayhem shook his head, looking as puzzled as the rest of them. "Maybe the scrawnies warned whoever it is that we're hard to kill and they're trying something different."

He snarled. Different wouldn't save them from dying. "It won't work."

Menace growled, fury and frustration in his voice. Strife knew exactly how he felt.

Mayhem turned from the monitor to look at them. His expression was as cold and hard as ancient stone. "Let them come. This is our home and we'll defend it."

Yes, they would. "To the death," Strife intoned.

"To the death," Menace repeated.

They came together to butt heads, the clack of horns punctuating the contact. "Good hunting," Mayhem said.

Then the three of them parted. The hunt had started. When they saw each other again, they'd have new stories to recount and more victories to celebrate.

Strife vaulted the railing and let himself fall half the distance to the ground before he extended his claws and caught the next branch that came within reach. He used it to slow himself down, twisting and jumping from bough to bough until he reached the ground. The moment his feet touched, he set off at a run. His territory wasn't far, but his home was on the far side of it, and he needed to go there first. If he was going hunting, he needed his weapons.

He ran hard, not wanting to waste time. It wasn't just his own territory he was protecting. It was his clan. The verexi never came themselves. They were too frail for combat, or even space travel. That's why they'd created the fa'rel in the first place. Strife and his brothers were intended to be the first of a new race of soldiers who could fight the scrawnies' battles for them.

That hadn't been the way it worked out.

Just thinking about it made the scar on Strife's left wrist itch and burn. It served as a permanent reminder of his captivity and the cruelty of the ones who'd created him. Every time he repaired a system or built something new from what little they had, he'd scratch the scar and smile to himself. They'd done this to him... and he'd make them regret it.

Maybe this time he'd manage to take the invader's ship before the assholes blew it up. Better yet, they could try for the main ship, which would be loaded with everything they needed—better weapons, better tech, and a working communication system. He was tempted to gather up a hunting party and go after that one now, but they had to deal with the smaller ships first. He couldn't risk leaving a threat at his back, and they'd all sworn to defend their territory. It was the best way to protect the entire clan.

The weather changed before he reached the enemy's landing site. The warm, sultry afternoon darkened as storm clouds rolled in, blotting out the sun. The air grew still and heavy as even the local animals sought shelter in preparation for what was coming.

He ran on. Rain didn't bother him, and while the storm was dangerous, it would also provide cover. The lightning and thunder would add to the chaos of battle, giving him an advantage. This was his world now. They were invaders, and they were not welcome here.

The terrain changed as he moved toward his target. The land flattened out a little, and the forest was broken up by meadows of fire grass. In bright sunlight, the plant looked almost like it was on fire, and even under the storm-dark sky it glowed like dying embers. Bysshe had told them it was because the plants had something called bioluminescence. The android was usually right about such things. Strife didn't care what it was called. He just appreciated the small amount of light it offered.

He held a small tracking device in one hand and checked it as he ran. It was the only one he'd managed to build from leftover scraps of technology salvaged from the ship they'd crash landed here. It detected power sources, and while its range was limited, it guided him toward the only power source around—the enemy's ship.

Lightning arced across the sky as he reached his destination, illuminating a small, oval vessel in the middle of a clearing. It was an odd design with no obvious engine or armaments and so small it couldn't have more than a single passenger. A scout, he decided. And not a very good one.

They'd set up camp only a few meters from their ship, and while the bright yellow structure matched the local flora with some success, it was all one shade. That didn't help it blend in. It was also lit up from inside, the warm light making it glow like a beacon in the gloom. Strife revised his earlier assessment. No soldier would be this careless. It had to be a trap.

He circled the camp cautiously. No one was outside, but someone was definitely inside the shelter. They didn't even try to avoid casting a shadow as they went about their business. Based on what he could smell, they were preparing a meal—one that carried the scent of chemicals and the loamy aroma of... *vegetation?* He shuddered in revulsion. Killing them would be an act of mercy.

A bolt of lightning shot down from the sky, the flash illuminating the entire clearing in brilliant detail. Two targets. One choice. Strife ignored the shelter and went for the ship. He'd disable it first and then deal with the scout.

He was almost to the ship when the first clap of real thunder pealed. Until then, it had been a distant grumbling, but not anymore. Strife grinned and resisted the urge to roar into the deafening noise. He felt exactly like the storm—primed and ready to explode.

Another noise caught his attention. Someone sobbed in fear. He hadn't heard that sound since his earliest years of captivity. They'd all slept in the same room back then, and sometimes one of them would cry out in their dreams, waking the others. It sounded like that... only different. The voice was softer but with a glittering edge of raw terror.

It wasn't a sound any soldier would make.

Strife turned back and approached the shelter. He drew his longest blade and held it high. Then he glanced up at the storm-black sky and lowered his arm. More lightning forked across the sky, leaping from cloud to cloud in brilliant arcs, closely followed by more thunder. The clouds opened and loosed a torrent of rain. It pounded the ground like a thousand small fists. He was drenched in seconds, the rainwater soaking his fur and running down the curve of his horns to drip onto his shoulders.

The noise came again and he moved toward it, suddenly consumed by a need to offer comfort to whoever made that sound. His fingers tightened on the grip of his blade, a silent reminder that he was here to mete out punishment to an invader. They'd come here to do harm to him and his clan. They didn't deserve compassion.

The next thunderclap was met by a terrified scream—a *female's* scream. He'd only heard such things on vids and recordings, but he was certain.

He dashed to the front of the shelter, half expecting to find the enemy waiting in ambush. The area was empty apart from a silver packet of uneaten food sitting outside the door. It was the same vile stuff he'd smelled earlier. It would seem even the enemy had some limits to what they'd consume. The partially open door made his next move clear.

He charged inside, adrenaline pouring through his veins with his entire focus on surviving the first moments of battle... only a fight didn't materialize. He found no obvious enemy. The only person in the tent was huddled in a corner, her hands clasped over her ears and her head bowed.

"Surrender and your end will be swift," he snarled before his senses could register the total lack of threat.

The female looked up then, her mouth open in a silent scream of shock. She scrambled backward, cramming herself as far into the corner as she could manage. In the buttery light of the glow-pod he could make out some of her features. Large gray eyes, golden-brown skin, and a heart-shaped face that would have been attractive if it weren't for the deep lines of fear etched into it.

"What species are you?" he demanded. He knew the name and description of all the verexi's allies. She didn't match any of them. In fact, she almost looked...

"Human," the female said. "So yeah, no one is going to care if you kill me."

He lowered his blade and then shook his head to clear the water from his eyes. They'd sent a human female. It didn't make sense. "Why is a human working for the verexi? They despise your kind almost as much as they do mine."

The female wrinkled her nose. "I don't work for them. Even I have *some* standards. I don't even work on their ships if I can help it. They smell disgusting."

"The verexi or their ships?" Strife struggled to follow

the conversation. He'd come prepared for battle... and now he was a little lost.

"Both, I guess, though their ships are always drones or AI piloted, so I've never met an actual verexi. Their ships smell nasty, like rotting lemons. Or what I imagine that would smell like. I've never seen a real lemon." She shrugged. "I don't get out much. This cruise was my first time off Nanu station. A chance to see the galaxy, you know?" The female dashed a hand across her wet cheeks and made a rueful, bitter sound. "Now that I'm out here, I just want to go home."

He sorted through her tearful babble and latched on to her last statement. This was something he could understand. "You can't go home."

"Of course I can. I just need to wait for someone to answer the distress beacon." Her voice softened to a desperate whisper. "Can't I?"

"This planet is a prison. Those who come here stay here. No one is coming to rescue you."

The female dropped her head, her shoulders slumping in abject misery. "I've died. I must have. I died and this is one of the nine hells."

3

_____

She had to be in one of the hells. She'd suspected it since the sky had gone dark and started to growl and rumble, but now she was certain. She'd died and the powers that be had sent her to whichever hell had huge, horned demons with gold fur and fangs.

"You're not dead yet." He took a step toward her and brandished the wicked-looking blade he held in one hand. "But you will be if you try anything. You are my prisoner. Understand?"

She nodded and slowly raised her hands, still dazed by the storm and the sudden arrival of what had to be the sexiest male she'd ever seen. Even if he was a demon of some kind. He was over two meters tall, with a powerful build and a body made from nothing but sculpted muscle and fur. He wore leather plates tied to his lower legs, a pair of leather straps that crisscrossed his body, and a skirt of some kind made from strips of hard, shiny leather that hung from a band at his waist and fell to mid-thigh. If this really was hell, at least it had eye candy.

Belatedly, she realized she was staring and remembered to answer him. "I'm the prisoner of a prisoner on a prison planet. Sure. Why not?"

"Stand up. Slowly."

She snorted with derisive laughter. "Honey, after the day I've had, *slowly* is the only way it happens." She was only in her mid-forties, but she felt every second of it after the events of her day.

It wasn't easy to stand up while keeping her hands in the air, but she managed it. That's when she realized just how *big* the alien was. Her head didn't even reach to his shoulder, and his biceps were as big around as her thighs. Water dripped from his horns, and his short, tawny fur was plastered to his skin.

He looked like an ancient forest god from human lore—one of the ones that seduced young maidens who ventured too far from home. She was as far from home as she'd ever been, but no chance in the nine hells did this male's plans include seduction of any kind. She was too old to believe in fairy tales and much too old for him. She had no idea what his age might be, but everything about him screamed that he was a male in his early prime.

Despite knowing that, Rissa took a moment to dry her eyes and tuck a few stray curls behind her ears. Personal pride required it.

The big male with the large, stabby weapon looked her over appraisingly and then asked, "What is your name and military rank or affiliation?"

She waved the fingers of her right hand at him to try and lighten the tension of the moment. "I'm Clarissa Aden.

Everyone calls me Rissa. No military rank. I'm a level-six ship's engineer working on Nanu station."

"Rissa. I am Strife." He looked like he was about to say more, but a deafening boom erupted overhead. This one was strong enough she swore the ground shook.

Terror crashed over her like an icy wave, and the last of her control shattered. The only thing scarier than the big alien interrogating her was the storm raging outside. She didn't know if instinct or insanity sent her flying into Strife's arms, but that's where she found herself. Her arms wrapped around his ribs and her face buried in the wet fur of his chest.

At first, he didn't move. His body was so still and hard it was like hugging a block of steel. Then something happened. It was like a part of her soul reached out to his and found something she hadn't known was missing. Her terror melted away in the heat of that connection, replaced by something even more consuming and primal. *Need.*

A shudder moved through his massive frame, followed by a low groan of desire that made her knees tremble. Heat pooled low in her belly as her nipples hardened and her libido roared to life like someone had thrown a match into a fuel tank. His scent filled her lungs—a subtle musk with notes of spice and wild places. She'd never smelled anything like him before, but it soothed her like it was an old and familiar friend.

Strife dropped the knife and then bowed his head over hers, his lips nuzzling her hair. A low rumbling sound that was almost lost in the storm rose from his chest, but she could feel the vibration as it moved from his body to hers.

She moved one hand from his back to his sternum, her palm pressed to his skin. Then she looked up at him.

His eyes were bright amber flecked with traces of black and gold, and she couldn't mistake the desire glowing in the depths.

"What's happening?" she asked, not sure which one of them she was asking.

Strife raised a hand to her face, his thumb beneath her chin with his fingers splayed across her cheek. "What are you doing to me?" he demanded.

"I'm not doing this. You are." And whatever he was doing, she didn't want him to stop.

"Liar." Something pricked the skin beneath her chin as he spoke, followed by more pinpricks across her cheek and jaw.

Rissa froze. It wasn't the knife. She'd seen it fall, so what was pressed against her skin right now? The answer came to her a second later. *Claws.* Strife had claws...

"Stop doing whatever you're doing and I'll make your end quick."

That was the second time he'd threatened to kill her, and despite that, she was still ready to climb him like a scaffold. What was *wrong* with her?

"I'm not lying. The only thing I am right now is terrified." And more aroused than she'd been in her entire life, but now didn't seem like a good time to mention it.

His eyes narrowed and then he inhaled deeply. His nostrils flared and his chest rose like a hydraulic piston being primed. "What are you afraid of?" He arched a brow. "Because it's clearly not me. I can smell that much."

Her cheeks heated to the point she probably could have

heated her dinner on one. "The storm. The noise." She uttered a desperate laugh that came out as more of a croak. "This whole fucking planet scares me."

"But I don't?"

She shook her head. "You do but only because you've threatened to kill me twice, and right now you could slice my face off with a twitch of your hand." Despite everything, it was easier to forget about the storm when she was with him.

"I won't do that." To her surprise, he raised his and let her watch as his claws retracted.

"Won't shred me or won't kill me?" she asked, trying to sound braver than she felt.

Strife smiled. It was a barely there smirk, but she saw it. "No shredding. If you are telling me the truth, I will not kill you either."

"I'd appreciate that. I've got a life to get back to. It's not much, but it's mine... I've still got things I need to do and family to take care of."

Strife's lip twitched again, this time into a silent snarl that showed one of his fangs. "Family? You have a mate?"

"What? No! No mate. I'd hardly be on a matchmaking cruise if I had a man at home already."

"No mate. Good. That's good." Strife relaxed, one hand reaching out to toy with a curl that had fallen over her face again. "You were on a cruise to find a mate? Are no males available where you live?"

His touch made her pulse skitter and jump like she'd been mainlining caffeine and pulling double shifts. She had to fight to focus on anything else, including forming words. "Uh. The cruise, yeah. It's a human-run company that takes eligible women to the territories of other species so we can meet and mingle." Once she started talking, she couldn't seem to stop.

"I wasn't doing that, though. I mean, I was on the cruise, but I won a contest, and that was the prize. I wasn't really looking for a mate. I mean, it would be nice, but you should see some of the females on this cruise. Well, the ones that were there at the start. They were beautiful, and they got snatched up quickly. By the time we crashed few of us were left. I guess you could call us the leftovers."

By the time she ran out of words, she was ready to throw herself under the nearest rock and hide. Babbling and describing herself as dating scraps was no way to make a good first impression. And that was after he'd seen her ugly-crying and terrified. Nukes and novas, at this point she should just borrow his blade and fall on it herself.

Strife looked at her with confusion, his fingers still tangled in her hair. He cocked his head to one side, his brow furrowed, which deepened the dark lines that ran from his eyebrows to his hairline. "You're saying that there are so many unmated females that you have to search for a breeding partner? I didn't realize your species was dying out."

Rissa decided that confusion was better than rejection and relaxed a little. "I'm not sure we're dying out, exactly. We're sort of the intergalactic version of a cockroach. No one wants us around, but we're damned hard to get rid of. It's just... guys like what they like, and some women don't tick the right boxes."

Strife's expression changed to one of utter bewilderment. "What boxes?"

She shrugged and hoped it made her look indifferent. "You know. Sexy. Flirty. Fun. Curves in all the right places and none in the wrong ones. Youth is important, too. Gray hair and wrinkles aren't sexy."

"Your hair has no gray in it. Only black and pretty little bits of white." He drew out a curl and let it wrap around his finger. She'd almost colored her hair before the trip, but in the end, she'd decided against it. Now, nestled in Strife's embrace with all his attention on her, she wished she'd dyed her hair and taken every anti-aging treatment the ship-board spa had offered.

"In this case, white and gray are judged to be the same. Both are considered unattractive traits."

"Like this." His voice went flat. He held up his other hand so she could see it. A ring of white hair encircled his wrist. At first glance, she thought it was another marking, like the dark lines around his eyes and above his brows. Then she looked closer and realized it was too rough to be natural.

She reached out and ran a finger gently across the back of his wrist. The flesh underneath was lumpy and thick. It was a scar. "No. This is a sign of strength. It means you were hurt but survived the injury. You overcame something."

He turned his hand and caught her fingers in his, his hand easily engulfing hers. "Has your life been easy?"

She didn't understand what that had to do with their current conversation, but she answered honestly and simply. She had to because most of her focus was on the way he held her hand and the warmth of his fingers against the side of her face. "Nothing in life is easy. Never has been. Never will be."

He nodded and lowered his head until his mouth was only a whisper from hers. "Then why would anyone think white hair is unattractive? It's proof you are a survivor."

She opened her mouth to argue, but no words came out. She had no counter to his statement and no desire to debate him on the topic. Not right now. Not when he was so close.

His lips brushed hers gently, and she gasped in surprise. Strife growled and kissed her again, harder this time. His mouth slanted over hers and his fingers tightened in her hair. He drew her head back, releasing her hand to wrap a strong arm around her waist and pull her tightly to him. She felt the hard planes of his body pressed against her softer curves.

The contrast of soft fur and rock-solid muscle intrigued her, as did the low purring sound he made as he plumbed the depths of her mouth. Even the flashes of lightning and claps of thunder faded from her awareness. His kiss consumed her, kindling desires and needs she'd denied herself too long.

For the last few hours, she'd done nothing but react to her rapidly changing circumstances. The engine failure, fleeing in an escape pod, the storm, and Strife's unexpected arrival. She wasn't really in control of her current situation, either, but she did have a choice. Granted, most of her choices today hadn't worked out too well. She should have had dessert instead of working out, she'd brought down the escape pod in the path of a major storm, and the ration pack she'd picked for dinner had turned out to be some kind of legume casserole that smelled like a sweating logaran with halitosis. She'd tossed it outside after one bite... and then the storm had broken. Mother Nature hadn't liked it either.

Throwing Strife out of her shelter wasn't possible, but something told her if she said no, he wouldn't force her.

Fuck it.

She rose on her toes and caught hold of the leather straps that crossed his chest, using them to pull herself up so she could kiss him back. She'd made her choice. She wanted this. Wanted him. Everything else could wait until after the storms passed, both the one outside the shelter and the one that raged inside her.

4

THIS FEMALE INTRIGUED and bewildered him. She spoke more than anyone he'd ever known, and many of the things she said about herself were unkind... and obviously untrue. Yet she seemed to believe them. It was confounding, and so was the way she made him feel.

He'd been fine until the moment she'd touched him. After that, his mind had refused to work properly. He'd even dropped his weapon. One touch from Rissa and he'd abandoned years of training. It had to be a trick of some kind.

But she hadn't attacked him. In her fear of the storm, she'd turned to him for comfort. *Him.* It was a new experience. The verexi feared their creations too much to even approach one of them unless they were restrained. He and his brothers had quickly learned that to show fear or weakness only made their brutal lives worse. They never showed fear or sought to comfort each other with more than a glance or a gesture.

Another time someone had offered him a few crumbs of

kindness and acceptance, and he'd been young and stupid enough to believe it. Their betrayal had left him with more than the scar on his wrist. It had left him wary of trusting anyone... even his brothers, the only family he had.

His instincts screamed warnings. This had to be a trap or a trick of some kind. He couldn't let her go. Not when she was clearly frightened of everything around her but not of him.

As she pulled herself up to kiss him, he stopped listening to anything but the voice demanding he take this female, comfort her, protect her, and give her so much pleasure she forgot about her fear.

His purr was louder than it had been since the first time he'd been given a pleasure bot to slake his adolescent lust on. He'd rutted with that thing for hours, but that had been a physical act. This... felt like something more. He wanted to bathe his cock in the heat of her body and listen to her cries of pleasure as he took her, and then he would hold her in his arms and keep her warm and safe until morning. He wanted to take her home and make her scream his name again while she lay in his bed, covered in his scent.

Her clothes were large, but the more he touched her, the more convinced he was that she was even smaller than he'd first thought. The loose-fitting pants and even larger shirt hid a lush, curvy body he wanted to see more of. Right now.

He sliced through the bright green fabric of her shirt with his claws and then pulled the tattered remains off her shoulders before letting it fall to the floor behind her. The color made the outfit useless in this place. She'd stand out like a beacon against the red and orange foliage, and the cloth was too thin to protect her soft skin. At least, that was the excuse he was going with. Not that he needed one. She was his prisoner. She would do what he wanted and wear what he gave her.

Her skin was a warm golden-brown that contrasted with the cool gray color of her eyes, though nothing was cold about the look she gave him as he stripped her bare. Her eyes were bright with needs that burned as hot as his own.

This glorious female didn't see him as something to be feared... but someone she desired.

The thought made his cock even harder and his balls tightened in anticipation. He needed to see more of her, to touch and taste her. It had to be some sort of temporary madness, and the only way he could think to overcome it was to embrace it now and see what remained when it passed.

Rissa's small hands moved over him, exploring his body as he explored hers.

When his hands found her breasts, she shivered and moaned softly, her own fingers moving to his chest so they were on his nipples. She tweaked one gently, and he growled as sparks of desire shot through him, sending a surge of need straight to his balls.

Fuck yes.

He let go of her just long enough to release the buckle that held his kilt in place. He shoved it over one hip and it fell to the floor. A few seconds later, more leather landed beside it as he shed the rest of his gear, though he left two knives strapped to his biceps... just in case.

"I have no idea what species you are, but damn, you are

incredible." The moment the words were out of her mouth, Rissa blushed and dropped her gaze to the floor.

"I am fa'rel. The verexi created us to be their soldiers. But I don't want to speak about that right now."

She gave a small nod but didn't look up. "What do you want to talk about, Strife?"

He growled and dropped into a crouch in front of her, deliberately putting himself back in her field of view. "We're not going to talk at all."

Her pants were so loose he didn't even need to use his claws to remove them. They slid down her hips with a light tug. She made a half-hearted attempt to catch the waistband as they fell away, but she was too slow. Instead, she tried to cover herself with her hands, concealing her stomach and her last remaining piece of clothing.

"Do not hide yourself from me." He caught her hands and drew them away, easily ignoring her attempt to resist him. "Why do you wear so many garments?"

"Uh. Because it's expected." She tried to gesture with one hand, but he still held it in his, and all she managed was a slight flutter of her fingers. "And uh, other reasons. Practical ones that I really don't want to talk about."

He looked up at her from his new vantage point, which allowed him to see her lush body in new ways. "These are your only clothes. Yes?"

Rissa gave a sharp little nod. "Yes."

"Good." He shifted his hands, gathering both her wrists in his left hand while unsheathing his claws of his right. He hooked two fingers into the waistband and tugged sharply. The fabric parted easily. A few more careful slashes and the pieces fell away, leaving her naked.

"You are too beautiful to cover yourself like that," he informed her. Then he leaned in to nuzzle his face against the rounded curve of her stomach. Lines fanned across her skin, covering her lower stomach and part of her hips. They were subtle, shimmering things, like delicate stripes.

"You have markings like mine." He touched one of the lines and then tapped the black stripe that ran from his brow to his hair.

"Those aren't like yours," Rissa said softly. "Yours are beautiful. Mine are just stretch marks."

"Stop that," he snarled. "You are my prisoner. What I say is."

He didn't like it when she argued with him, especially when she put herself down at the same time. "I like them. They're pretty. Just like you."

Rissa looked down and to one side, not meeting his gaze. "Thank you. You're very pretty yourself."

"I am me." He wasn't the largest of his brothers, or the fastest. He was a good hunter and a better soldier. That had always been enough. But he had to admit. He liked that this little female thought he was attractive. He would reward her for that.

He caught her hands in his and placed them firmly on his horns. "Hang on. I don't want you to fall."

She wrapped her soft hands around his horns where they rose above his hair. "Why would I fall?"

He didn't answer her. She'd understand soon enough. It only took a few seconds to catch hold of one of her ankles and lift her leg over his shoulder.

"Oh. Oh!" she exclaimed as comprehension struck.

Then she laughed, a joyful belly laugh that made parts of her jiggle in fascinating ways.

He arched a brow in question, staring up at her from his position on the floor.

"Sorry. I just realized I'm having the best dream of my life. That's what's going on. I'm not dead. I'm dreaming."

She thought this was a dream? Strife's lip curled up in a faint snarl. "Challenge accepted."

Rissa made a startled noise that only got louder as he moved in close and nuzzled the soft curls that hid her pussy. He parted the flesh with his fingers, every movement slow and deliberate. He understood what to do, but he'd only seen it done in the vids their captors allowed them to view. The pleasure bots he'd been provided with had an instructional mode. He'd never interacted with a real female before. He wanted to remember every second of this experience and prove to her that this was no dream.

He breathed the scent of her arousal deep into his lungs. It reminded him of the flowering vines that grew around his home. Their delicate blooms only opened at night, filling the air with their spicy-sweet perfume. That's what she was... his blossom.

He ran the pad of his thumb over the little nub of flesh hidden within her folds, and Rissa gasped, her hands tightening around his horns.

Yes. He wanted to hear her make that noise again. He wanted her to moan and whimper, to make every sound of pleasure she was capable of. Most of all, he wanted to hear her cry his name as he made her come. Tonight, he'd make that happen. Tomorrow, once this strange fever had passed, he'd decide what to do with her.

Keep her forever.

The thought of claiming this female made him purr with pleasure, and that... gave him an idea.

He licked and lapped at her tender flesh, letting the sweet nectar of her arousal flow over his tongue. Every touch made her moan and shiver, and when he glanced upward, he saw she was staring down at him, her eyes half closed with pleasure and her lips in a soft "O."

His cock was so hard it ached and his purr was louder than he'd ever experienced before. It might have been her enjoyment, or maybe it was the fact she trusted him with her body this way. He didn't know, and right now, he didn't care.

He sucked her clit into his mouth and she cried out as the vibrations of his purr flowed from his tongue to her body.

"Oh hells. Yes. That. Please don't stop. I..." She trailed off, the words fading into a needy moan as he slipped a finger into her tight channel. Soon he'd have his cock inside her instead of his fingers, and he'd get to feel the hot, slippery heat of her body wrapped around him as he fucked her. His female.

By all the stars above, he liked the sound of that.

It didn't take him long to learn what she liked best. He used that knowledge to bring her to the edge of orgasm and then held her there for a time, licking and teasing her until her hands shook and her knees wobbled.

Then he let her come. She called his name as she bucked and writhed, grinding herself against his mouth and chin. He managed to get one arm around the back of her thigh and a hand planted firmly on the lush curve of her ass before her orgasm knocked her off balance.

The knowledge that he had brought this female to her knees made him swell with pride. And when she slid, boneless and sated, into his arms, he knew exactly what this meant. She had surrendered to him.

She was his now, and he had no intention of letting her go.

5

Rissa knew all the words to describe what she'd just experienced. She'd read them in her stash of romance novels enough times... but she'd never understood what they meant until now. Orgasmic. Ecstasy. Mind-melting. She'd thought they were ideals to strive for but never actually achieve.

Nukes and fucking novas had she been wrong about that. They were achievable... if you found the right male for the job. Apparently the right male for her was on a prison planet, and the only way to meet him was to crash land on said fucking prison planet. She didn't really believe in guardian angels, but if she had one, they had clearly taken up day drinking.

Strife helped her untangle from him, and then she found herself curled in his lap, her head nestled against his shoulder as he cradled her in his arms. It felt almost as good as the orgasm.

Almost.

He didn't give her much time to recover. He caught her by the hair, gently drawing her head back until she was looking up at him. She had a moment to admire his handsome features and marvel at the perfect line of black fur highlighting his golden eyes. Then his mouth was on hers, and her world went up in flames again.

His kiss was eager and demanding, too hungry to be polished and too possessive to be gentle. She liked it more than she cared to admit. He kept kissing her as he lowered them both to the floor. The move left him stretched out beneath her with her legs straddling his hips. His cock was a steel bar pressed against the seam of her pussy. He was long and thick—and holy hells, were those ridges? She ground her pussy against him to confirm what she suspected. Yep. Ridges. Whatever species he was, when the biologically compatible female population of the cosmos learned about them, they were going to be the most popular males in the universe.

That thought almost made her pull away from him. Why was he doing this? Why her? Compared to him, she was a candle flame burning next to a star. He could do so much better...

Then she remembered where she was. A prison planet. How many females were here? Any? If not... that explained his eagerness.

Strife growled. "Why did you stop?"

Rissa hadn't even noticed she'd stopped kissing him. She opened her mouth to tell him some minor white lie, but the truth barged out first. "How many females are on this planet?"

Strife's brow creased. "None. Why does that matter?"

Being right sucked vacuum sometimes. "Because I didn't understand why you wanted me... this. But I get it now. I'm not what you want. You just lack options."

"No. I don't want to want you at all. You might be the enemy. You might be a trap of some kind. You must be because the moment you touched me..." He shook his head and then raised his hips so his cock slid along her slick flesh. "You were not what I expected to find, night blossom, but that doesn't matter anymore."

His hands landed on her hips and lifted her off his body, just enough for his cock to slide into position.

She gasped and tried to stay focused on his words and not his actions. "Why not?"

He thrust upward, bringing their bodies together in one smooth motion that left her seeing stars. "Because you are mine now."

"What? Nooo-my-stars..." her protest changed to a moan of raw need as he took her again, withdrawing and then surging into her. The ridges of his cock made her quiver and gasp with every move he made.

"Yes," he groaned, one hand lifting from her hip to cover one of her breasts.

She lost the ability to form words or even think. All she could do was feel... and it felt amazing. Rissa fell into the golden light of his eyes, basking in the admiration and desire she found there. It felt like how she'd thought basking in sunlight would feel, warm and welcoming.

She caught hold of his wrists and used them for balance as she grew brave enough to take a more active role. She rolled her hips, matching the rise and fall of his body so they moved as one. Strife groaned as his cock swelled, the ridges she'd felt earlier becoming more prominent. He filled her completely, every stroke making her nerves sing with pleasure.

He let her set the pace, watching her with half-closed eyes so full of passion and fire she felt like a goddess. He wanted her. Desired *her*. Something deep in her soul reached out to him, wanting everything he could give her.

It was madness but of the best kind, and she let it consume her.

Her inner walls flexed and fluttered against his cock, striving to give him as much pleasure as he gave her. As his cock thickened, it was almost too much for her, pushing ecstasy close to the boundary of pain without ever crossing the line.

"So tight," Strife groaned. "So good. I never imagined..."

His compliments were like little hits of some premium pharma, taking her higher and making her feel better than she had in her life.

She leaned forward, planting her hands on the floor beside his head so she could lean down and kiss him as they fucked.

He growled into her mouth, his tongue tangling with hers, and the next moment she was on her back with Strife looming over her. His pace quickened, his thrusts becoming more erratic as they chased the tail of the comet, racing each other to the pinnacle of pleasure.

She reached it first, and her back arched against him. Every ridge and line of his cock added to the tsunami of pleasure that crashed over her as she came.

Strife lasted a few moments longer and then he threw back his head and roared as his orgasm hit with all the fury of a sudden storm. His cock pulsed and jerked inside her as he emptied himself into her body. None of her partners had ever shown this much passion while they were with her, and she discovered she liked it... a lot. This was hot and real and primal, and sexy as hell.

Then the ridges of his cock flared, swelling him so much he was locked inside her, and she tumbled into another completely unexpected orgasm. This one was even more intense. She couldn't do anything but ride the waves of pleasure and cling to Strife, her cries muffled against his mouth as he kissed her again and again.

Rissa's first coherent thought when she finally recovered was that as far as choices went, sleeping with Strife had to be the best one she'd ever made.

They were still locked together, and any movement sent fresh aftershocks of pleasure zinging through her body. Strife held himself above her, his kisses gentle and accompanied by the soft rumble of what she thought of as his purr.

Her hands moved over every part of him she could reach, exploring and memorizing the details for future replay. His fur was soft and sleek, and it felt like stroking satin. Only beneath the softness were hard lines of muscle and sinew.

"You are magnificent," she said, not aware she was speaking aloud until Strife chuckled in response.

"So are you, blossom." He seemed about to say more, but then his jaw tightened and his smug expression turned into a perplexed frown.

He shoved himself high enough he could look at his chest, and she instinctively followed his gaze.

Three lines appeared like slash marks crisscrossing his chest and growing darker as she watched. They started at his shoulders, crossed over his sternum, and then ended near his flanks.

"What have you done to me?" Strife demanded.

"Nothing! I have no idea what's happening." Rissa's wrists tingled, and she rubbed at one with the other hand, her attention still focused on Strife's chest. It wasn't until the tingling intensified that she finally looked down. She had a matching set of marks on her wrists, smaller than Strife's, but otherwise identical. Three black lines curved around her wrist and crossed each other at the top.

"What the fuck?" She scrubbed at the mark, but nothing happened. It didn't hurt, or feel any different than her normal skin, but something had definitely changed.

She had stripes, for fuck's sake. This was why humans should stay away from planets! Random acts of striping weren't a problem on any space station she knew of.

Strife eased their bodies apart gently, despite his obvious concern about what was happening.

He gathered his weapons as he got to his feet, and within seconds he stood glaring down at her, his blade back in his hand. At least he kept it pointed at the floor. "What are these marks? What have you done?"

"I could ask you the same question," Rissa retorted. She didn't bother trying to stand up. He'd tower over her either way, and she didn't trust her legs to hold her right now. They were still unsteady after all the orgasms.

He touched a clawed finger to his chest. Then he

appeared to notice something and spread out the central three fingers of his hand, placing an extended claw on each line. It was a perfect match.

"See? I told you this wasn't my doing. Those marks fit your claws." She held up her hands and waggled her fingers. "No claws here. Whatever this is, it's your weirdness, not mine."

He caught her wrist in his hand and then pulled her to her feet so he could look more closely at it. She had no say in the matter. In fact, he barely seemed to notice that he'd lifted her off the floor one-handed.

"See?" she said, not bothering to try and pull away.

"I see." He let go of her hand and stepped away from her. "I see, but I don't understand."

"That makes two of us, which doesn't make sense. This isn't something humans do, so it's got to be you. So, why don't you know what it is?"

Strife sighed and scrubbed a hand over his face. "Because none of us know anything about what we are. The verexi created us in a lab. We're not a species. We're an experiment... one they deemed a failure."

"A failure?" she spluttered. "In what way? From where I'm standing, you look pretty damned perfect."

"We were intended to be soldiers under their absolute control. They got the first part right." His lips curved up in a hint of a smile, and he touched the band of scar tissue on his wrist. "But they could never find a way to control us for long."

She reached out to him, but he took another step back, out of her reach. "I'm sorry, Strife. I cannot imagine what that must have been like for you." She sorted through the rest of his statement. "You said this place is a prison. Did the verexi put you all here? And how many prisoners are there? Are they all like you?"

"They pretended to bring us here so we could have more freedom. It was a lie. They planned to kill us, but someone warned us and we fought back. Our ship crashed, but me and my clansmen survived. Now, the verexi send mercenaries to try and finish the job. So far, they've all failed." He cocked his head to one side. "Do you truly not know any of this?"

She looked him square in the eyes and said, "I don't know anything about you. I don't even know where I am. Everything I have is from the escape pod's emergency supplies." Rissa shook her head. "I'm no mercenary. Hells, I'm afraid of almost everything on this planet, including the weather."

Reminding him that she'd been terrified out of her mind when they'd met was embarrassing, but it was better than having him think she was his enemy. Right now, he was her only real chance of surviving more than a few terror-filled days. If he'd told her the truth, no one would come to rescue her or anyone of the others.

Rissa's heart ached at the thought. Her fathers wouldn't know what happened to her... they'd think she died. Unless the company that owned the *Bountiful Harvest* tracked down the signal. Surely then there'd be a rescue attempt. The passengers and crew were mere humans, but the ship was owned by a large multisystem corporation. There'd be an investigation at the very least, and they'd want to salvage the wreck. She still had a shot at being rescued... for her.

But what about Strife and his brothers? They'd done nothing wrong. They didn't deserve to be here either.

Take him with you, a little voice whispered in the back of her mind. It was a crazy idea, but that didn't make it any less tempting. The question was, how could she make it work?

6

STRIFE DIDN'T KNOW what to believe. When it came to Rissa, nothing made sense. He needed to get out of here. Away from this female with her soft voice and lush body. She was muddling his mind somehow, distracting him from what he needed to do. "I'm going outside to make sure the storm didn't do any damage to the shelter or the escape pod. You will stay here until I return."

Rissa nodded, and he couldn't tell if she looked relieved or disappointed. She was the most confusing creature he'd ever met... not that he'd met many. Maybe that was the problem. He'd only dealt with the verexi, his brothers, and Bysshe.

Bysshe. Yes. Talking to him was a good idea. The android had been their teacher, their mentor, and their only ally at the research station where they'd been held most of their lives. He needed to talk to Bysshe and then introduce her to Rissa. He'd been built by humans. He'd know if she was telling the truth.

All this ran through his mind as he backed away from

Rissa. When he got to the entrance and moved the flap aside, she spoke again.

"I'm going to grab another meal pack. They're self-heating rations. Nothing special, but it's food. Would you like one?"

No one but his brothers had offered to share their food with him before. But could he trust her?

She spoke before he could, obviously reacting to something in his expression. "I won't open it. I'll just activate the heating function."

He felt a little foolish. He'd just taken this female and made her scream in pleasure. His scent covered her soft skin, and he could smell her on him, too. He'd done that, yet now he thought she might poison him? He needed to find his focus, fast.

"I would like that, but something with meat in it, please. I do not eat plants. Especially whatever was in that meal you prepared earlier. I don't blame you for tossing it out."

"The packet claimed it was a legume stew." She wrinkled her nose. "I've worked on backed-up recyc-units that smelled better. I'll find something with meat in it for you."

He'd meant to leave but found himself lingering to say one more thing. "Thank you, Rissa. I won't be long."

When he ducked outside, he was met with a different scene than before. The gloom of the storm was gone, but twilight had fallen. It would be fully dark soon, and the first stars were already visible. He could still hear the rumble of distant thunder, and the air still had that close, cloying feeling he'd learned meant another storm was likely before morning.

His bare feet squelched in mud as he moved, and the wet grass clung to his lower legs, soaking him to the skin. He'd have to remember to use some of that grass to clean his feet off before going back inside.

Broken branches littered the ground around the tree line, but that was the worst of the damage. The shelter was intact. He'd have to come back for it later. It was far too valuable to leave behind.

In fact, he'd have to bring some of his brothers out to help him carry everything here back home. Until now, the mercenaries had always managed to fly away or destroy their ships before the fa'rel could reach them. While the pod would never fly again, it would be useful for parts, and the rest of the supplies were invaluable, too. The scrawnies had never intended for them to survive the initial trip to bring them here. The supplies they'd provided turned out to be expired, out of date, or generally useless. The only thing they didn't understand was why their captors had sent any supplies at all.

Once he'd finished checking for damage and threats, he turned his attention to the real reason he'd come out here. He needed to destroy the emergency beacon in the escape pod. It didn't matter who she was or what brought her here. This was verexi territory, and anyone who came to investigate that signal would have the same orders as everyone else who came here: Kill anyone you see.

The moment he opened the panel to the pod's controls, his scar started to itch. It happened every time he worked on anything electronic. He hadn't worn the control device since the moment they'd decided to rise up, but his body still remembered the pain and reacted to the memory.

Strife ignored the sensation and overrode the instinct to pull his hand away. Bysshe assured him that it would get easier as time passed. Strife was starting to doubt it. Why was it that every time he wanted something, he ended up losing it and being punished for daring to want anything?

He'd wanted a friend... and they'd betrayed him. The scrawnies had implanted him with tech that allowed him to interface with all sorts of systems and then punished him for learning to use it too well. He'd been forced to watch and feel every second of the procedure where they'd deactivated his implants. He'd still been young then, and he'd passed out before they finished patching him up. He'd awoken to discover a new cuff fastened to his wrist, directly over his incisions.

Vata, the one he'd stupidly believed had been his friend, had been there to explain.

"If you come within reach of any system, this band will punish you. The only time you will be permitted access is when you are under direct supervision. Only then will the cuff be deactivated."

Young and injured as he was, Strife had already learned one of life's harshest lessons. The galaxy only contained two kinds of beings—family and the enemy. Vata had proven to be an enemy, so Strife did what he'd been trained to do.

He attacked.

After that, the technical training stopped, and Strife spent more time in isolation than any of his brothers but Rage. They'd left messages for each other on cell walls and played games one move at a time, some of them lasting for months.

Rage hadn't lived long enough to taste freedom, so Strife was determined to enjoy it for both of them.

It was the work of only a few minutes to destroy the beacon beyond any chance of repair. Rissa had said she was a ship's engineer. He had to be sure that she couldn't fix the beacon. All their lives depended on it.

The packet of food had disappeared from the front of the shelter by the time he returned, and something far more savory filled the air. *Meat.*

He'd used a handful of grass to clean most of the dirt from his feet before going inside. "I'm back," he announced as he moved the flap aside and stepped through.

Rissa was crouched near the back of the shelter with her back to him, and his first instinct was to growl and tell her to never do that again. It was more proof that she was who she said she was. No soldier would ever make that mistake, especially not when they were deep in enemy territory.

She'd wrapped herself in a blanket of silvery material and secured it with a knot above one breast. It fell to mid-thigh and covered too much of her body for his liking, but he recalled that unlike the verexi, some species wore clothes for no other reason than to hide parts of their bodies. Rissa turned and smiled at him, and this time he clearly saw the relief in eyes. She was pleased he'd returned. A female was *happy* to see him.

She gestured at two identical food packs set out on the lid of a medium-sized container. "The food is almost ready. I found something that claims to be beef in some kind of sauce. It smells better than the last one, at least."

"It does," he agreed. "What are you doing now?"

Her lower lip vanished between her teeth, and she

looked almost sheepish for a moment. "Uh. Well. I assume we're staying here tonight, so I made up the bed."

She shifted to one side to let him see. Two bedrolls were laid out side by side on top of what looked like some kind of inflatable sleeping platform that hadn't been there before. One had a single silver blanket laid out neatly, perfectly aligned with the walls of the tent with a small, flat thing that must be some sort of pillow at one end. The other had a similar pillow and two blankets, one unfolded already and the other sitting carefully centered at the foot of the bed.

"That one's yours," she said, pointing to the one with two blankets.

Strife took one look at the layout and shook his head. "No."

"No?" She looked back at her handiwork and then reached for the single blanket on her side. "You want this one, too?"

"No! Not that. You should take the blankets. You have no fur to keep you warm. I do."

Then he took another look at the setup. "Why is there space between the beds?"

"Uh, because after what you said before, I thought you'd want to be away from me, you know, since you think I'm the enemy."

He caught the faint burr of annoyance in her words and hid a smile. His little blossom had thorns. *His.* The thought caught him off guard, but it didn't feel wrong. In fact, it felt good. And true. Fucking hells, what was wrong with him?

He glanced down at the marks on his chest and made a decision. "We sleep together. I will keep you warm far better than any blanket."

Her eyes lit up and the skin on her cheeks turned a deeper shade of gold. "You don't need to do that. I mean, I know we..." she ducked her head and waved her hand in an agitated gesture. "But I get that you're probably not a snuggler."

He had no idea what that word meant, and his translation matrix didn't either.

"Snuggler?" he repeated the word slowly, trying to mimic the sound she'd made instead of relying on their translators to do the work.

"Someone who likes to snuggle up. Uh, cuddle?" Rissa wrapped her arms around herself and squeezed. "Like a hug that lasts a long time."

"I've never done that," he admitted. "Do you like snuggling?"

She blinked. "Never? No one ever snuggled you as a child? Or as an adult? I mean, I'm sure any woman in the known worlds would be happy to snuggle with you. You are insanely handsome and apparently a nudist... I cannot believe you've never snuggled with anyone."

He set down his weapons and then gathered up the two meal packs and brought them over to her. He sat down beside her and then offered her one. "There are no fa'rel females, and the scrawnies are asexual." He tore open the pouch and let the steam escape as he spoke. "You are the only female I have ever met."

Rissa dropped her unopened packet on the floor. "I am? But that means..." She uttered a horrified groan and devoted her entire focus to retrieving her food and carefully pulling a single-use utensil from the side of the pouch.

He followed suit and then dipped it into the contents

and lifted it to his nose. It smelled edible, but he was still waiting for Rissa to finish her statement.

"I don't understand your reaction. Why are you upset that I have never seen a female before?"

He ate as he waited, suddenly ravenous. The food was tasty enough, though a little sweeter than he liked. Why would someone ruin perfectly good meat by adding sauce to it?

The silence stretched out for several seconds before Rissa answered. "Because that means you can't have had sex before. So that was your first time..." She shook her head. "It should have been special."

That confused him. "What makes you think it wasn't?"

"Because someone like you should be with a female as good looking as you are, and closer to your age."

He snorted. "Who makes these rules? Why should it matter if we are the same age or what you look like? I think you are pretty. Therefore, you are pretty." He waved his hand for emphasis. "What does it matter what someone else thinks?"

"I was struggling to believe you were really brought up in a lab until you said that..." Rissa gave him a sad little smile. He didn't like seeing her sad, so he put the packet and utensil between his teeth, leaned over, and picked her up.

She squeaked in surprise but didn't protest as he settled her onto his lap. Then he took the packet out of his mouth and went back to eating.

"Why did you do that?" she asked.

"Because you were unhappy. Now eat and explain to me what made you sad."

"Has anyone ever told you that you are annoyingly bossy?" she asked, ignoring her meal.

"I am not bossy. Wait until you meet my brothers. They are..." he stopped and scowled. The idea of introducing Rissa to his clanmates didn't appeal to him. She was *his*.

"They're what? Now you're the one not finishing sentences," Rissa teased.

"Stubborn. Difficult. Arrogant. I have decided they don't get to meet you. Not yet."

Rissa scoffed. "Can you hear yourself? First you say you're not bossy, and then you announce you've decided things for me without even asking what I want. That is textbook bossiness. I've worked in shipyards my whole life. Believe me, I know what bossy sounds like."

"Eat your dinner, blossom. Then you can explain why you think I was wrong to choose you as my first."

The more she insisted they shouldn't be together, the more he wanted to argue with her. She *was* beautiful, she was not too old for him, and by all the stars that burned, she was his. His prisoner. His prize. His blossom.

7

———

Rissa kept herself busy while Strife was gone. She'd prepped the food packets and made the beds because she needed to do *something*. She always thought better when her hands were busy, and she didn't have much time to sort out the tangled mess of her thoughts and feelings.

Why had she responded to him the way she had? What was with the markings they both had now? And why had it stung so much when he'd pulled away from her again?

The answer to the last question was the easiest. Rissa knew herself well enough to recognize what had happened. She'd been a foundling, abandoned on the station by her parents or whoever had been caring for her until then. She had no memories of them, and her records indicated she'd been taken in as a child of seven or eight months old. She was raised in a multi-species orphanage on Nanu station, the only human child among the ever-changing population.

Her fathers had adopted her when she was nine and given her all the love and stability she'd ever dreamed of, but part of her still remembered being alone and unwanted.

That part wanted to please everyone all the time, and when she couldn't, she felt rejected and blamed herself. That's what was happening here, but knowing that only took away some of the sting.

"Get over it," she told herself, careful to keep her voice to a whisper. She'd learned that saying things aloud helped her follow through, but she didn't want Strife to hear her. He had enough doubts already, no sense in adding to them.

She hadn't let herself acknowledge her fear that he wouldn't come back until he reappeared. Her survival depended on him, and maybe her happiness did, too. She couldn't tell. Those emotions were still too tangled up to make sense of yet.

Their conversation had only tangled things up further and added several more layers in the process. Strife was a virgin! Or he had been until today. She'd seduced an innocent... or maybe she'd been seduced by one, but that didn't seem right.

When rescue came. *If* it came, she'd lose him to someone younger and prettier. It was inevitable. If he stayed here, she'd never see him again. Another loss. But if she wasn't rescued and spent her life here, would any of it be real? Did he want her, or was it just a lack of options? She suspected it was the latter. She'd liked vat-grown proteins until she'd tasted real meat, and after that, the artificial stuff had never tasted quite right.

She mulled that over while also trying to explain to Strife about the expectations and rules of a society he'd never been part of. Neither course of action was going well.

Then he'd made it even more difficult to think by lifting

her into his lap so she was skin to fur against his very hot, very naked body.

"Eat your dinner, blossom. Then you can explain why you think I was wrong to choose you as my first."

He stared at her intently until she took a mouthful of food. This was far better than the stew, and she ended up taking several more bites before she spoke again.

"You weren't wrong. I mean, both of us felt the attraction. It's just, in my society, there are expectations. Older women don't get involved with younger men, and those who do are usually judged for it. And someone as attractive as you would have your choice of females, so it would be unusual for you to choose to be someone who wasn't uh..." she floundered as she tried to think of a word that wouldn't make his translator malfunction. "Breathtakingly beautiful."

"No one here will judge you. More likely, they will be jealous of me." He scowled. "And try to take you from me. You are not to go with any of them. You are mine."

"They'd take me as their prisoner?" She didn't like that idea at all. As confusing as all this was, she trusted Strife to take care of her.

"They'd take you as their female. If they want one, they will have to find their own. I found you first. All this." He gestured around them. "Is mine. And so are you."

"You don't even trust me not to poison you. Why would you want me?" The words were out of her mouth before she could stop herself.

"I don't know why, but I do. Very much." He set aside his meal pack and leaned down to kiss the top of her head.

"I think that's what these marks are for. They mean you belong to me."

She held up her wrist and looked at the marks again. They hadn't faded. In fact, they might be even darker now. It was impossible to be sure, but she thought so. "So this means we're supposed to be together, and that we should trust each other?"

"I think so. But if you do anything to try and harm me or my clan, I will know the marks were a trick, and you are my enemy."

"That's not how trust works," she protested.

"It is for me. If you want to keep my trust, you must earn it."

She shifted in his lap, leaning back until she could see his face. "Then the same goes for you. You've threatened me three times now. How am I supposed to trust you when you keep doing that?"

He gave her a crooked little smile. "Don't try to kill me or my brothers and *never* feed me vegetation. Other than that, you have nothing to fear from me, night blossom."

"I've never killed anyone in my life. I like to fix things, not destroy them." She paused a beat and then asked, "How many times have you killed, Strife?"

"Not often. Three mercenaries who came here to kill us, and I terminated every bot and droid aboard the ship that brought us here. They were programmed to kill us at some point before or after we landed and then cover it up somehow. We never learned the details.

"So, you've only killed in self-defense." That made her feel better. Everyone had the right to live their life. If anyone tried to take that away, their own lives were forfeit. It was the way things were.

Strife shrugged, but his shoulders stiffened as he tightened his hold on her. "No. Once I killed someone because they betrayed me. I don't regret their death, either."

"Be-betrayed you? How? Did they serve you a salad or something?" Fear made her voice brittle and her attempt at a joke fell flat.

He raised his arm, the one with the scar that left his fur white. "They are the reason I have this scar. I thought they were my friend, but they were working with my enemy all along."

Well, that explained his trust issues. Rissa reached for his wrist. When he didn't pull away, she gently placed her hand over the scar. "I am not your enemy, Strife. I won't betray you. I promise."

He twisted his wrist and captured her hand inside his. Then he raised it to his lips, kissing her fingertips first. He drew her index finger into the heat of his mouth and sucked on it. Desire welled up inside her again, overflowing the walls she'd built to try and contain it. Strife's cock hardened beneath her, and his purr rumbled from deep in his chest. She could feel the vibration of it travel through her finger, and it flowed all the way to her suddenly throbbing clit.

"Are we done eating?" she asked.

His golden gaze locked on hers as he released her finger from his mouth. "You are, for now. I am not. I need to taste you again, blossom."

Heat washed over her, making her cheeks burn, but she spoke her mind anyway. "I think I'd like to eat, too."

"You want food instead of me?" Strife looked almost insulted.

Rissa shook her head and laughed. "No. I want to taste you while you taste me."

He groaned and nodded. "Yes. Show me how this is done. I want that, too."

She kissed him softly and then set aside her unfinished meal. Without a word, she got to her feet, her fingers already working to undo the knot that held her blanket in place.

If he'd never been with a woman before, the least she could do was show him what she knew. Someday, some lucky female would thank her for it, even if they didn't know her name.

Strife prowled after her, his movements so predator the hairs on the back of her neck rose up to warn her something dangerous was coming for her...

Holy hells, she hoped so.

She dropped the blanket at the foot of the bed and then stretched out on her side, one foot flat on the floor and her head propped up on one hand. She could only hope it looked sexy and alluring, but she had no way to be sure.

Not until Strife growled loudly and then pounced on her.

She laughed in delight as he destroyed her carefully arranged beds to create a nest in the middle of the sleeping platform. Then he drew two of his fingers through the soaking folds of her pussy, teasing her clit just enough to make her gasp.

"Time to feast," he said.

She guided him into position and then took his thick

cock into her mouth, humming softly as he groaned and shuddered with pleasure.

"Again," he demanded, parting her lips with his fingers to expose her clit.

She took him deeper into her mouth and laved the length of him with her tongue. Bossy he might be, but this was one order she was happy to obey.

Not that she would admit it to him.

8

WAKING up next to someone else was a new experience for Strife. So was sleeping through the night without nightmares of his former life plaguing his dreams. He'd woken up contented and at peace with Rissa nestled against his side.

It was another sign that she was meant to be his.

He stayed in bed as long as he could, watching Rissa sleep and recounting the details of her life she'd shared with him before she'd fallen asleep.

Her life in the orphanage wasn't so different from his own childhood in some ways. She'd experienced loss and loneliness too, though hers had ended when she'd been adopted by her fathers. One was human, like her, the other was a hybrid—part human, part trazin. The trazin were one of the founding members of the Galactic Legion, warriors and skilled traders who were respected and feared by all other species. The verexi considered them dangerous, which meant he and his brothers had studied their tactics, technology, and physical attributes in detail.

They were larger even than the fa'rel, with dagger-sharp horns and a war bellow that could reportedly shake the ground beneath their enemies' feet. The idea that such a creature had raised Rissa fascinated him. She had followed in her fathers' footsteps and become an engineer like them. The human specialized in robotics while the trazin hybrid was a ship's engineer like Rissa. What would it have been like to learn skills from caring parents instead of viewscreens and videos?

Eventually he got up, trying not to disturb her as he rose. He left the tent, did a quick sweep of the clearing, and then went a short way into the woods to answer nature's call.

By the time he returned, Rissa was awake and was once again wearing one of the blankets as a garment. He didn't understand it. Why did she insist on covering herself?

"Good morning," she greeted him, her voice warm. "Now you're back, I'm going to uh, pop out for a moment. If you hear me screaming, please come save me from whatever is trying to eat me for breakfast."

"Do not go far and watch for grass serpents. You will be safe. Or I could go with you if you wish?"

"With me? Um, thank you, but no. I won't be long."

She moved past him, letting her hand brush his hip as she did so. At the doorway, she paused, took several deep breaths, and then stepped outside, her head down and her eyes staring at her feet.

He could smell the bitter tang of fear. He didn't like that she was afraid, but he appreciated her decision to face her fear alone. His blossom had courage, even though he didn't understand her fear.

Rissa had already cleared away their bedding and the sleeping platform had been deflated. There must be a control mechanism for it somewhere. Once this equipment had been brought home, Rissa could show him how it all worked. The rainy season wasn't too far off, and an inflatable, waterproof shelter would have many uses.

He looked through the remaining meal packs, but eventually gave up. The pictures were unhelpful and his translation matrix was keyed to verbal languages not written ones. Bysshe was programmed with a number of human languages, though. With the android's help, it wouldn't take him long to learn to read and write Rissa's language. He considered himself the smartest of his brothers, but all of them were more intelligent than the scrawnies ever knew. Strife scratched at the scar on his wrist. Showing off for Vata that day hadn't just cost him his implants and earned him years of punishment. It had almost cost his brothers their lives. It had taught him a valuable lesson, one he needed to remember right now. Everything good always came at a price.

Rissa felt like a very good thing to him, but there were some costs he wouldn't pay. His own happiness wasn't worth his clanmates' lives. As much as he wanted to trust her, he couldn't. Not yet.

The thought was like an icy dagger driven deep into his chest.

When Rissa returned, she looked a little unsteady, but the scent of fear had faded.

She walked into the middle of the shelter, placed her hands on her hips, and looked at him inquiringly. "So, what happens now?"

"We go home." He thought that was obvious. The shelter had done its job, but his home was more comfortable and far safer. He could think of at least three land predators that could tear through the shelter's walls without much effort, though he wasn't going to mention them to Rissa just yet.

Her complexion turned an alarming shade of gray. "You mean your home? How far away is it?"

"It took me more than two hours to run here yesterday. The morning passes quickly. If we walk back, we won't reach our destination until late afternoon."

She looked at him almost pleadingly, the confident female who had demanded what happened next replaced by one who looked like she might collapse at any moment. "All that time outside?" Her voice cracked. "I can't do that, Strife. Can't we stay with the pod?"

He was by her side in less than a second, drawing her in close to his body so she could lean on him while his arms held her steady. "We can't stay here. Come home with me, Rissa. I have a safe, comfortable home, with a solid roof, sturdy walls, and even electricity."

That drew a reaction. She tipped her head back so she could look up at him, her expression puzzled. "How the hells do you have power out here? Is there a city you forgot to mention until now?"

"No city. We do have hydroelectric generators, though. Wind turbines, too." Did she think they lived like primitives? The verexi hadn't given them much, but the fa'rel were survivors. They'd built what they needed out of what they had available. He'd show her when they got back home.

"How solid is the roof of this house of yours?" she asked.

"Very. I spent the last rainy season dry and comfortable beneath it."

"I don't care about getting wet," she said. "I just don't want to see the sky. It's... too big."

"Water doesn't bother you, but air does?" Strife found this whole conversation confusing, but at least she seemed calmer and more like herself.

Rissa made a strange sound somewhere between amusement and frustration. "Small amounts of water don't concern me. I can even pretend that the rain is just a really big shower. Until this trip, I'd never set foot on a planet, and the two I visited before crashing here scared the hells out of me. Weather. Animals. Open spaces. I'm not used to any of those things. I've lived my entire life inside a station with layers of protection and failsafe systems, most of which I know how to repair."

"And that worries you." Now he understood.

"It terrifies me. Back on the ship, when the alarms went off, I was concerned but not scared. My first thought was to get to engineering and offer to help. Then someone shot at us and we had to abandon ship. Since then, I've just been trying to stay alive and cope with one crisis after another."

"Your ship was attacked?" She hadn't mentioned that before.

Rissa's brow crinkled uncertainly. "I think so. I've never been in combat, but that has to be what made us crash. Our hyperdrive failed, and we fell back into normal space. That was normal enough. Not ideal, but it happens. Then all hell broke loose. Lights flashed, alarms sounded, and doors sealed shut to prevent atmosphere loss. Then something hit us hard enough to make the floor shake. After that, we were all ordered to abandon ship."

Strife had a good idea of what must have happened. "You're right. You were shot down. From what we can tell, the verexi have defense platforms protecting this place. The only ones who can get past them are their own mercenaries."

His female's expression changed from uncertain to shocked and then furious. "The fucking verexi shot us down? We weren't even in their territory! Those assholes. Wait until the legion finds out. There will be several kinds of hell to pay."

He let her finish venting and then clarified things for her. "You are in their territory, Rissa. This entire system is. From what we were able to glean from the ship's database, we're situated near the border between their space and the logaran empire."

"We can't be. Well, no. Apparently we can be, and we are. But I shouldn't be here. We were never supposed to come near verexi space. They consider us a lower-level lifeform with minimal value. Why would a human matchmaking cruise go near their territory?" She frowned. "Someone fucked up. Like, big bang level of fuckery."

"I think you're right. But the fact is you are here now."

"I am, but don't you see? I won't be for long. The company who owns the Harvest will come looking for it, and once they figure out where we are, they'll get permission for rescue and salvage operation. The legion recognizes us as sentient life with certain rights. The verexi will have to allow it. I need to stay close to my escape pod so they can find me." She paused and took a breath. "My fathers... I don't want them to think I'm dead."

Strife grunted and tugged at one horn in frustration. Rissa still didn't understand her situation, but now he understood why. If someone had told him he could never see his brothers again... that they'd spend the rest of their lives thinking he died and he couldn't tell them otherwise. He wouldn't want to accept it either. "You can't do anything to change the facts. The scrawnies don't allow anyone to come here. They brought your ship down because it was too close to a prison planet. Anyone responding to an emergency beacon will most likely be another mercenary unit with orders to destroy evidence and silence any witnesses." He caught her chin and made her look him in the eyes, needing her to understand. "No one is coming to rescue you, Rissa. If they come at all, it will be to kill you. And they won't detect your beacon. I destroyed it last night."

Pain, confusion, and anger shone in Rissa's eyes. "You... what? Last night? Why?"

He snarled, his temper fraying. "Because that beacon wouldn't just lead them to you. It would lead them too close to my brothers. Yours is not the only life I need to protect!"

"I never asked you to protect me!" she shot back, pushing at his chest with her soft hands, but he wasn't ready to let her go.

"You didn't have to ask. Since the moment you touched me, that's all I've wanted to do. You belong to me, Rissa Arden, and I do not need your permission to protect what is *mine*."

"How can I be yours when you don't trust me? If I put

all logic and sense aside and run with this idea that these marks mean we're supposed to be together, it's still the worst possible foundation to build a relationship on that I can think of. Finders-keepers is a children's game, not a basis for falling in love with someone."

His translator struggled with some of her words, but he got the gist of what she was saying. He even agreed with some of it. It didn't change a damned thing, though. "I was raised in a lab and treated as an experiment. I don't know anything about love or relationships. I just know that I am not leaving here without you. If I do, you will die, and I won't allow that."

Her reaction surprised him. She laughed. It was sharp and discordant, but he sensed real amusement too. "I'd almost forgotten what males your age are like. So convinced you can change the course of stars through pure will. Even if I do come with you, there's still every chance I could die, whether you allow it or not."

He wanted to fold his arms over his chest, but to do that, he'd have to let her go. Instead, he straightened up to his full height, tall enough his horns brushed the roof of the shelter. "You will never question my ability to protect you again. I can, and I will."

As he spoke the words, he felt the truth in them, and that awareness made them into something more... a promise.

But would this confusing, glorious female understand what he meant?

9

———

Rissa wanted to stay angry because it was easier than dealing with all the other emotions clamoring for her attention. Fear, grief, and embarrassment were all there, demanding their turn. Embarrassment was the loudest of the bunch. Her control had slipped and she'd gotten emotional. Worse, she'd let Strife see her like that—all vulnerable and messy. Even worse, she'd gone into a tailspin even though he was right. Destroying the beacon was the smart choice, especially for him. Her life wasn't the only one at stake here.

Her reaction to his declaration had been more barbed than she intended, but it would allow her to regroup and redirect the conversation.

At least, that's what she thought until he straightened his spine, squared his massive shoulders, and looked down at her like she was something small and squishy, which from his point of view was probably an accurate description.

Then he spoke, and his words made her pulse race and her insides melt into a puddle. "You will never question my ability to protect you again. I can, and I will. I'm a skilled hunter, soldier, and survivor. I *will* keep you alive. More than that, I will protect you, provide for you, and make you scream my name in pleasure. Repeatedly."

She believed every word. "Is that a promise?"

Strife's smile returned and his golden eyes glowed with something she couldn't name. "Yes, blossom, that's a promise."

She placed both of her hands on his chest and slowly moved them up his body, to his shoulders, his neck, and then his face. She didn't stop until the fingers of one hand were tangled in his hair, and she held on to one of his horns with the other. "Thank you. I know I wouldn't last more than a few days on my own. I'd be stupid to pretend that wasn't true. But I also meant what I said. Relationships are built on strong foundations made up of things like respect, trust, and honesty. I know that because it's how my fathers make their marriage work. I don't know what this is between us, but..."

Rissa paused and gathered up her courage. Things were about to get emotional and messy again, but this time it felt like the right thing to do. "If I have a choice, I'd like to try to make this thing between us real and good. Something that makes us both content, if not truly happy."

She had no idea what Strife's reaction would be, but she'd needed to say it. If staying here with him was the only option she had, she didn't have many choices left to make... but she would choose to find what happiness she could.

He didn't answer her in words, but he leaned down to claim her mouth with his, and his kiss was hot, hungry, and all-consuming. She decided that meant he agreed with her.

Then she stopped thinking completely. It was so much easier to let go and enjoy the raw physical pleasure of being in his arms.

He kissed her until her head spun and her lungs burned. The points of his fangs grazed her lips and tongue, and she felt the prickle of claws gliding over her skin, an erotic counterpoint to the power of his kiss. His cock was a heavy bar of steel caught between their bodies, and she ached to have him inside her again.

He purred as they kissed, the vibration rolling through her, soothing and arousing at the same time.

When he raised his head, they were both panting softly, and the knots of fear and grief she'd had before were almost gone by the time she could think clearly enough to notice them at all.

"As tempting as you are, blossom, we should go. Otherwise I'll spend the entire morning fucking you right here, which is foolish when I have a comfortable bed waiting for you back home."

"Your home, which is going to take us all morning to get to." How the hells was she going to manage that? Knowing her fear was irrational and foolish didn't make it any less real. In time, she'd work through it the same way she'd overcome some other fears she'd had, but that wouldn't help her today.

"Trust me." Strife's voice was surprisingly tender.

She had no idea what he could do to help her, but she nodded once in agreement. What else could she do?

Strife carried everything out of the shelter, managing it with enviable ease and speed. She kept her eyes on the ground and made it into the trees without too much trouble.

Under the canopy of leaves it was easier to ignore the broad expanse of blue sky she knew was up there. It had taken time to adjust to working in the vast emptiness of space, too. She'd been frightened, disoriented, and nauseated for the first few weeks, but at least then she'd had a vac-suit keeping her alive and offering a protective layer between her and the cold void.

Being on a planet was different. There were no bulkheads, barriers, or walls here. No protective gear to wear and no way to know what was happening in the surrounding environment. She didn't know how to predict weather, detect threats, or even figure out what time it was.

Once she explained to Strife how to deactivate the shelter, he'd taken over the job, leaving her to pack a few items into a small shoulder bag she'd found among the supplies. She went through the rations and picked out the ones she thought would be the most palatable. She took the glow-pods that had illuminated the shelter last night along with a couple of basic, multipurpose tools and a canteen of water. After she added the blankets, the bag was more or less full. She was about to close the container and seal it again when she spotted something else—an emergency transponder, this one small enough to be portable. It would be a backup to the escape pod's beacon, dormant but available in case the pod was destroyed or the survivor had to move some distance from their landing site.

It was small enough to fit into her bag.

She stared at it as her mind raced. It wasn't active. It was no threat to Strife or any of his clan unless she activated it, and she wouldn't do that unless she had a good reason. It was insurance. That was all. A last-ditch measure if it turned out Strife wasn't who she thought he was. She wanted to trust him, but she had no way of knowing if anything he'd told her was true. Taking the beacon was a sensible precaution. Right? And she couldn't tell him about it, or he'd destroy it just like the other one.

Rissa reached for it, stopped, and then let her breath out in a hiss as she snatched the little white and orange orb. She didn't want to imagine a situation where she'd actually use it, but she hadn't expected to find herself crash landed on an apparent prison planet, either.

She shoved it beneath the blankets and fastened the shoulder bag closed just as Strife approached, pulling the container that contained the repacked shelter.

She glanced up and then back down again as soon as she saw blue sky over Strife's shoulders. "I'm done here."

"Good. I'll secure the gear we're leaving here and then we can go."

She put the bag over her shoulder and retreated to the nearest tree, keeping her back pressed to it as Strife sorted out the containers. He checked the seals on them both and then wedged the smaller one into a gap in a tangle of tree roots that covered part of the forest floor. Then he pulled the larger one that contained the shelter in place in front of it.

"Discouraging any curious animals from poking their snouts where they don't belong?" she asked.

"Lizards, mostly. The little ones won't be able to do much to material this durable, but they'll probably try to gnaw on the edges anyway. Black Fangs are the ones I'm worried about. They're big enough to tear these containers open, but they hunt by scent." Strife inhaled deeply and then shook his head. "I can't smell the meal packs inside, so they shouldn't be able to either."

"Charming name. Do I want to know how big these creatures get?"

Strife shot her a lopsided grin. "Probably not."

Rissa groaned. "Planets suck. Have I mentioned that yet?"

"You'll get used to it."

She didn't know what to say to that, so she stayed quiet.

Strife noticed. "When we first arrived here, I wasn't thrilled about it, either. Freedom was amazing, but the only time I'd spent outdoors was in an exercise yard. The lab they kept us in was on a small moon with minimal oxygen... or anything else. At first the noise drove me crazy. It's never quiet here, and lifeforms are everywhere."

Rissa managed a rueful smile. "You're making this place sound worse by the second. Maybe we should go before I decide to reactivate the shelter and hurl myself inside, never to leave again."

He cocked an eyebrow. "I don't recommend that."

She raised her eyes and waved a hand in his direction, trying to look unconcerned. "I know. I know. If I do that, you'll just get bossy and make me do it anyway."

Strife moved to stand in front of her. "Are you ready to go?"

Rissa swallowed hard and then nodded and pushed away from the tree. "I'm ready."

"Good. Then give me your bag, turn around, and close your eyes."

She had no idea what he had planned, but at this point, she didn't have anything to lose. She handed the bag to him.

He placed the strap over his own shoulder and then made a motion with one finger, indicating she should turn around.

She obeyed and tried to ignore the little thrill of excitement that chased down her spine as she turned her back to him.

A hand on her shoulder stopped her once she faced away from him. Anticipation and curiosity made her pulse race as she waited for something to happen.

"Trust me, blossom. That's all you have to do," Strife murmured, his mouth so close to her ear his breath was a warm caress across her skin.

He moved, and a moment later something cool and soft covered her eyes and settled over the bridge of her nose. He tied it once and then tightened it slightly before asking, "Comfortable?"

"Yes. But I have to ask. Is blindfolding me really your plan to get me to your place? How am I going to walk if I can't see?"

Strife finished securing the knot at the back of her head and then turned her around to face him, his hands on her shoulders to keep her steady. He didn't answer her until he'd run his fingers around the edges of the blindfold, checking for gaps she might peek through. "You're not walking, blossom. I'll carry you."

"You can't! You said it took you hours just to run here. You can't lug me around this forest that long. I'm too heavy."

He kissed the tip of her nose. "You are not. And if you say that again, I will be insulted."

"Don't say I didn't warn you," she muttered. Did the fa'rel have anything like a chiropractor in residence? After trudging through the woods carrying her and their gear, he was going to need one.

He ignored her comment and scooped her into his arms. Being blindfolded, the motion disoriented her, but she kept her focus on Strife and the feeling passed, though she assumed it would return the moment he started walking. As foolish as she felt, though, the blindfold did help. So did being back in his arms.

"Hold on to whatever you like, but avoid my blade. It's sharp and I don't want you hurt."

She spent a moment getting comfortable, laughing as she found the hilt of his sword rising off his back and the smaller knives strapped to both his biceps. She ended up folding one arm across her stomach and leaving the other resting lightly against his chest, her fingers closed around one of the leather straps that crossed his chest.

"Are you ready?" he asked.

"Would it matter if I said no?"

He chuckled. "Not really. But if you are uncomfortable or need me to put you down for a rest, just say so."

She opened her mouth to say something sarcastic about him putting her down *now*, but he stopped her mouth with a soft kiss.

"That won't work, blossom. Not yet."

She sighed in resignation and gave a little nod. "Then I guess it's time we went home."

Strife didn't say anything. He just set out... not at the walking pace she'd expected, but at a run.

It wouldn't take them all morning to get to his place after all. She wasn't sure if that would turn out to be a good thing or not.

10

Strife's pride was stung. Did Rissa think he was weak? He was strong, fit, and had more than enough endurance to carry her. Clearly, he needed to take her to bed when he got home so he could show her just how fit and capable he was.

Yesterday, the idea of sharing his home with someone else would have sounded like insanity. When he and his brothers reached puberty, they'd become increasingly territorial, to the point that their captors had to keep them separated most of the time, only allowing them to interact with one or two of their brothers and only for short periods of time.

When the scrawnies had stuffed all of them into the cargo area of the ship that brought them here, they were certain their experiments would tear each other apart long before they reached the planet. They'd been wrong... but only because he and his clan had fought against their nature instead of each other.

These days, they all lived on their own. Close enough to help each other and stay connected, but they each had their own territory. The only time they were all together were the monthly gatherings at the crash site, where they exchanged news, remembered their fallen, and drank copious amounts of Bysshe's fermented fruit concoction.

It was also the only time any of them consumed vegetation. The thought made him smile. He'd ask the android for some of the liquor for Rissa. She ate plants. In fact, he'd have to ask Bysshe for some of the fruit and other things he grew. Strife struggled to understand how a species could be so delicate they needed to eat more than meat to survive. What were the humans missing that they had to consume leaves and twigs?

He loped through the forest, one part of his attention on the female curled up in his arms and the rest of him taking note of the footing, the terrain, and any possible threat.

They were almost halfway when Rissa spoke for the first time. "I don't want to sound ungrateful, and the blindfold is keeping me sane, but..." She trailed off.

He stopped running and set her down gently. He held her against him, aware she might have trouble balancing after being carried and blind for so long. "Do you need to rest?"

"I'm okay. But I wish I could see something. I have no idea where we are or what anything looks like. Are we even in the forest anymore? What have you been jumping over?"

"Tree roots and rocks." He looked around and found a likely spot for what he had in mind. "I'm going to pick you up again, but only for a few steps. Then I think we can take that blindfold off for a while."

"Thank you." She leaned into him and nuzzled her cheek against his chest. That small gesture nearly broke him. He had a sudden urge to wrap her in his arms and never let go again.

No one had ever treated him the way she did. He never imagined anyone ever would... not until her.

He carried her to the base of a massive tree and got them both settled in a nook between two roots that rose half a meter above the ground. He had his back to the tree, and she had her back to his chest.

"I'm taking the blindfold off. Don't look up until you're ready."

She huffed out a soft laugh. "I don't plan on looking up at all."

He drew the cloth over her head and set it aside. There hadn't been much left of her shirt after he'd shredded it last night, but there'd been enough to create the blindfold she'd worn.

Rissa raised her head slowly and then gasped. "It's beautiful here."

They were so deep in the forest that the canopy of red and gold leaves blocked the sky from view. The sunlight was filtered through the foliage, dimming the light slightly but giving it what he'd always thought was an attractive glow.

"The trees are huge. Much bigger than the ones near the shelter," she commented.

"You were at the edge of the forest in an area we think must have suffered a fire some years ago. Those trees are younger than the ones you see now." He paused and then added. "At least, that's what Bysshe and the rest of us think. We have no way to know."

"I guess you don't. Planets don't come with maintenance logs or manuals."

They sat in comfortable silence for a few minutes while Rissa looked around and asked questions about what she saw. The big roots rose above the ground, tangling around parts of other trees and large, moss-covered rocks.

Eventually, Rissa dared to look up, and he heard her make a small sound of relief when she couldn't see the sky. "Is it like this all the way back to your home?" she asked.

"It is." Strife thought he knew what she was thinking, but he didn't want to push.

"Then I can stop wearing the blindfold. I know it's stupid, but seeing the sky triggers my fear. Logically I know that a layer of leaves isn't going to make any difference, but..." she shrugged.

"Fear isn't logical," he said, his gaze automatically dropping to his scarred wrist. The device that inflicted such pain each time he'd gotten to close to a computer system was long gone, but the reflexive response hadn't gone away.

"You're fucking right about that," Rissa agreed. "And I didn't even know I had this fear until I set foot on my first planet. They warned us it happened sometimes, but I thought I was tougher than that." Her laughter had a glittering edge like jagged ice. "Apparently I'm not."

"We all have fears we need to face. Anyone who claims they're immune to fear is either lying or has never done anything with their lives." Rage had told him that during one of their last conversations before he was killed in an escape attempt. He was the oldest of their clan, an earlier version of the fa'rel, or so the verexi claimed. Strife had never noticed any real difference, but he was a soldier, not a scientist.

Rissa relaxed, her body softening against his. "Well, after this, no one is going to say I've led a boring life... short, maybe, but not boring."

"Are you doubting my ability to protect you? Again?" he asked, growling just enough to punctuate the last word.

"Nope." She actually twisted her head to look up at him, her eyes alight with amusement. "If I live through this craziness, you can take at least half the credit. Maybe more, depending on what happens."

"Nothing will happen to you." He'd die first.

"So you keep telling me." She patted his thigh. It was a friendly gesture, but his brain interpreted it very differently. He wanted to turn her in his lap, bring her down on the already hard rod of his cock, and distract them both from these deep thoughts. He resisted, but only because he'd rather have her in his bed, where he could keep her safe and well-pleasured for hours. Possibly days.

"I guess we should get moving. We won't be able to go as fast now that I'm walking," she said.

They both got to their feet, stretched, and gathered up their few belongings.

"You're not walking." He pointed to a nearby root. "I took us a shorter way but one full of obstacles you'll struggle with. I will carry you."

"Holy hells. You've been jumping over *those*? You made it seem easy! At least, that's how it felt."

"It is easy for me, but I was made for this." He gathered her close and smiled down at her. "You were made for other things. Like sheathing my cock."

One dark brow rose toward her hairline. "I can cook, too. And fix damned near anything. I'm not just your personal sex toy." Her tone was light, but he detected a slender thread of warning woven around it.

She didn't like being reduced to a single purpose, which was fair enough. Neither did he. "You're right. You are much more than that, blossom. But when I have you in my arms, I can only think about one thing."

"You're insatiable." Her smile widened, and it was like witnessing the sun come out from behind the clouds. "And thank you. It's hard to think straight when I'm in your arms, too."

"Soon we'll be home, and neither of us will have to think."

He lifted her, gave her a few moments to settle, and then set off at a run again.

They hadn't gone far when he heard the piping call of one of the local predators. It was a warning cry and was quickly picked up by several more of its kind. He slowed to a walk, trying to identify what direction the noise had come from.

"What is it?" Rissa asked in a low whisper.

He answered in low tones that wouldn't carry far. "Tusk-hoppers. Lizards about half a meter tall, small tusks on their lower jaw. They're pack hunters. We must be close to a nesting site. That's the only time they get this aggressive."

"I haven't even seen one yet. How do you know they're getting aggressive?"

"Listen." He listed his head toward the source of the noise even as he turned away from it.

More cries rose from the trees behind them, and he saw several of the creatures watching from the shadows of the underbrush.

"That piping noise? That's them?"

"It is. If you ever hear that sound, you must determine where it's coming from and immediately walk away. They won't follow. They're just protecting their nests."

"Do you hunt them?" she asked.

He shook his head, his lip curling in remembered disgust of the one time they'd attempted to consume that species. "Their meat is tough and has a bitter flavor. It's also too much work to remove the venom sacs so the meat can be safely consumed. We leave them alone."

"Venom sacs?" Rissa's voice was tinged with horror and she shuddered hard enough he felt it.

"As I said, they are predators. One or even a few bites wouldn't do much harm, but they hunt in groups, and if each of them managed a single bite..."

"I get it. I'm also going to have nightmares about it for weeks. Ugh. Why couldn't I crash on a planet with marshmallow plants, fluffy, harmless animals, and rivers of chocolate?"

"I have no idea what marshmallow or chocolate is. I take it these are more foods made from plants?"

She laughed. "I think they were originally, but I don't know for sure. If they ever existed, they'd be on Earth, and I've never been there."

"Earth?" His translation matrix must be glitching because it seemed as if she'd called her planet "dirt."

"It's the original planet my species came from. I know, not a very inspiring name. Some humans call it Terra and claim they are Terrans instead of humans." She shrugged as if it didn't matter to her.

Strife didn't understand her attitude. When they were younger, he and his brothers would talk for hours about what kinds of DNA the verexi had used to create them. They had no home planet, no history, and no ancestors. "You don't care what your species is called?"

"We are who we are, no matter what we call ourselves. Besides, few of us are left. We thought we were heading out to conquer space and shape the galaxy in our image. Then we got out here and discovered others had beaten us to it. One of my dads used to say that humanity brought a rock to a plasma cannon fight."

The image amused him. "From what I know of your history, that seems accurate. Though we didn't study your species much. The verexi wanted us to focus on what they considered their greatest enemies."

"And from what I know of their history, that's a long list. No one likes them much," Rissa said. "I've met many species in my life, and all of them seemed decent enough. I mean, every group has their designated assholes, but in general, we're all just trying to survive and protect the ones we care about."

That fit with what he'd seen on the entertainment shows they'd been allowed to watch sometimes, but not with what the verexi had told them. The scrawnies feared everyone they believed were physically or technologically stronger and dismissed all others as being beneath their notice... including humanity. He suspected that was a mistake. Rissa was afraid, but that hadn't stopped her from doing what needed to be done to survive.

Once they were clear of the hoppers, he broke into a run again. He was eager to get her home.

"How many things on this world are dangerous?" Rissa asked.

"Many. But you have no need to worry. You just have to remember that the most dangerous thing out here is *me*."

11

———

Without the blindfold, the journey to Strife's home was much more interesting. Rissa made sure not to look up too often. If the canopy overhead thinned out too much, she closed her eyes until the light dimmed, telling her they'd passed into deeper cover.

The rest of the time, she drank in the view. Everything was fresh and vivid—from the colors of the flora to the scents that filled the air. It smelled like the carefully maintained conservatory back home, but here it was all so much *more*. Flowers. Trees. Plants. The soft moss that covered almost everything like a living carpet. Then, there were the sounds. She'd been too busy trying to survive to pay much attention to her surroundings yesterday, but today she heard everything. The wind in the leaves, the flap of wings that had to belong to some kind of avian analog, and the steady buzz of pollinators as they went about their tiny lives. This place was full of life, and that awareness comforted her a little.

If they could live here, so could she.

They stopped for a quick break at some point, but Strife was clearly eager to get home, and she was curious to see what his place looked like. He'd mentioned it had power, but what sort of structure was it? She'd seen vids and images of all sorts of colony-style construction. Most were little more than sturdy boxes that stood one or two stories high, but those were prefabricated buildings shipped and assembled on site. Whatever Strife and his clan had created to live in, the design would be limited by the need to use local materials.

Her engineer training wanted to see what they'd come up with and how they'd managed it. Her heart wanted to see Strife's home so she could get a feel for who he really was.

She wanted him to be the male she thought he was—protective, honest, and honorable. Maybe his home would give her more clues as to what kind of male he was and what her future might look like if she stayed here... with him.

The next time he stopped, she wasn't sure at first why. All she could see were more trees and rocks in every direction. "My home is just beyond that stand of trees. I've cleared the surrounding area, so some sky will be visible. I thought you should know."

"I think I can manage it so long as I don't have to look up," she said.

"That... might be a problem. Come. I'll show you."

He set her down and then took her by the hand, leading her along an obvious pathway that led through the woods and brush. The light brightened as they neared the tree line, the golden light of the sun heating the air and adding new depths to the colors she saw. Even in the light covering of her makeshift dress, she was sweating a little.

They stopped a few steps before the edge of the clearing. Several small lean-to-like structures were scattered around base of a massive tree. All the structures were rudimentary but functional. Judging by the smell, one was smoking... something. She couldn't tell if it was animal hides, meat, or something else. The scent was faint enough she guessed whatever fuel the fire consumed was spent or close to it. Another building at the far end of the clearing held what looked like bladed implements of several kinds with a large work bench made of roughly hewn planks placed nearby.

"Where's your home?" she asked, still scanning the clearing as if she could have somehow missed something that large.

"This is the part that might be a problem. See the large tree in the middle?" Strife pointed to the giant as wide around the base as a booster engine port.

"I do." Was his home inside the tree? Beneath it?

Strife stepped in behind her, wrapping both arms around her and drawing her back against his chest. "Look up."

She groaned. "This better be worth it."

It was. As her gaze rose, she noticed very un-treelike protrusions standing out from the trunk in a rising spiral. Stairs. The tree had stairs, landings, and a rope that acted as a sort of handrail. Branches as thick around as her escape pod, and some even bigger, stretched out and upward. In the center of all this was a platform, and on that platform was... holy hells. "You built your house in a tree?"

"We all did. Most of the predators can't climb that high, and during the rainy season we're safe from flooding."

While that made sense, it was also the strangest thing she'd ever seen, and that included a short stint repairing and customizing pleasure droids for Nanu station's busiest brothels. "It's a tree. How is that stable?"

"It's a very large tree," he pointed out in a tone as dry as a stale ration bar. "The tree supports the platform, and the platform provides a stable foundation for the buildings. Come. I'll show you."

She eyed the staircase that wound around the trunk. It was a lot of stairs. "And here I thought I wouldn't have to do any cardio today," she quipped.

Strife lifted one hand to cup her breast through the blanket she wore in a style somewhere between a post-shower towel and a sarong. "If you wish exert yourself, I have a better suggestion than climbing stairs."

Her stomach exploded with butterflies and as need sizzled through her veins. Her clit throbbed and her nipple hardened beneath his fingers.

"You like that idea." He nuzzled the side of her neck. "I can smell how much you want me, blossom." She could feel his cock against her back, so hard it had parted the protective leather thongs that made up his kilt.

"And I know you can feel how much I want you. Come. It's time you saw your new home."

It turned out to be relatively easy to cross the open area between them and the tree. All she had to do was let herself get distracted by the big, sexy male walking beside her. He held her hand like a gentleman, but nothing was civilized about the carnal words coming out of his mouth. He described everything he wanted to do to her in vivid detail, and by the time they reached the shaded area at the base of the tree, she was flushed, sticky, and ready to jump him right then and there.

Whatever this was between them, it wasn't fading. In fact, it was getting stronger the longer they were together. She was so screwed... and that realization didn't scare her as much as it should have. It was more proof she'd lost what was left of her marbles... or maybe she was losing her fear instead.

The climb was surprisingly easy, though the air was now oppressively warm. The solid platform might have been made of wood, but she saw conduits, wires, and junctions that made it resemble a station bulkhead, at least enough to fool herself if she didn't look too closely. It also blocked her view of the sky, and by the time they were halfway up, she felt more relaxed than she'd been since the first alarm had sounded yesterday.

She stopped on a landing to look around and indulge her curiosity. They were close to the bottom of the platform, and several narrow catwalks ran from the stairs to provide access to the infrastructure above her head. "Batteries?" she asked as she pointed up to a cluster of wires.

"Not as many as I'd like. The scrawnies didn't leave us many, and the main ship needs quite a few to power the systems we managed to repair."

That got her attention and she turned back to look at Strife. "You repaired the ship? Can she fly? What still runs?"

"We did what we could, but she'll never fly again. She slammed into a hill and triggered a landslide that partially buried her. We can use the med-bay in emergencies, and we have access to the ship's databases and navigation systems."

"Comms?" she asked. "If there's anything left, I might be able to get communication running again. That would change everything!"

He shook his head. "The verexi stripped out the entire comm system before we were put on board. There's nothing to repair."

"Well, shit. Wait! The *Bountiful Harvest* is still out there." Guilt and horror slammed into her as she realized she'd forgotten about the others. All this time, she'd been focused on her own survival.

"We'll find the crash site and recover everything we can," Strife said.

"And save anyone still alive?" Nukes and novas, she hoped the others had made it. "Hope was in a pod like mine. We need to find her!"

"My brothers left the same time I did. Your pod landed in my territory, so I went to you. Mayhem and Menace will have found the pods that landed in their areas. Your friends will be with them."

"There were two others?" She had no idea who could be in the third pod, but at least she wouldn't be the only survivor.

"Yes. The ship you were on went down some distance away. It will take time to get there, even for my brothers. If they're not already on their way, they will be soon."

"And then maybe we can send a message and let everyone know we need rescuing." She was thinking aloud, constructing a plan, just the way she always did.

"No!" Strife snarled, his voice harsh. "You don't need

rescuing, Rissa. *I* rescued you already. You are safe now. I will protect you."

"You rescued me, yes. But I'm talking about getting off this planet and back to somewhere with a sealed, regulated environment, no weather, and where nothing with the words like tusk or fang in their name are trying to kill me."

"You want to leave?" Strife's voice was as raw as she'd ever heard it, and she realized too late her mistake. "This place, yes. You..." she shook her head, not ready to put her feelings into words. She was falling for him hard and far too fast.

"Come on. Let's go inside. Then we can talk about this." She turned away, not paying attention to her footing, and stumbled over a board set slightly higher than the ones around it.

She staggered and flailed her arms to regain her balance, and Strife lunged, catching her before she came too close to the edge of the landing. Once she was steady, he let her go and stepped far enough away she knew he was still angry with her. Just not pissed enough to let her fall.

"You look flushed and unsteady," he observed. "When was the last time you drank anything?"

"Back at the shelter before you packed it up."

He grunted, unslung the bag she'd packed from his shoulder, and opened it before she realized what he was doing. "You need to drink before we continue."

"No! I'm fine. It's just a little..." She didn't get to finish her sentence before he found the beacon. His expression hardened, transforming him into something bestial and dangerous.

"What. Is. This?" he demanded as he pulled out the small sphere.

Instinct made her take a step back and raise her hands in front of her, palms out. "A portable beacon. But it's not active."

"Why?" he snarled, holding it out to her. "Why would you do this?"

"Because I barely know you and I know nothing about your clan brothers or anything else about this place. What if they want to hurt me? What if you were lying to me?"

"I don't lie," his fangs flashed as he spoke, and his voice had a low, dangerous edge to it. "I swore to protect you, and I would have."

He whirled and slammed the beacon into the trunk of the tree with enough force to send chunks of bark and polymer flying. Another blow and the beacon came apart in his hand, broken beyond repair.

I would have. His words repeated over and over inside her head. Would have. Past tense. *Shit.*

"Strife." She said his name and then stopped. She didn't know what to say next, and she wouldn't beg. She'd been protecting herself, and she wouldn't apologize for that.

He set her bag down on the landing and then shot her a look she couldn't decipher. Too many emotions were at play, and none of them were good ones. "Stay here. Rest. Eat. If you damage anything, I will kill you. If you leave, I will hunt you down and kill you."

"I won't—"

He was gone before she finished speaking. One second he was on the landing, the next he'd leaped out into space. She raced to the edge in time to see him leap and bounce from branch to branch, using them to slow his descent. He landed perfectly and then vanished into the forest without looking back.

"Fuck." She muttered a moment later. "Fuckity-fuck-fuck. That couldn't have gone much worse."

Defeated, sad, and suddenly weary, Rissa picked up her bag and trudged up the last flight of stairs. She needed food, water, and time to think. At least he'd told her to stay here. If he'd been truly done with her, he'd have sent her packing. That had to be a good sign... right?

By all the hells, she hoped so.

12

———

He'd done it again.

Strife tore through the forest at a flat run, letting the exercise purge the worst of his fury. He needed to think clearly, and he couldn't do that yet.

Rissa had betrayed his trust, and that knowledge burned like acid, sizzling at the edges of his mind. For the second time in his life, he'd trusted someone he shouldn't have... and put his family at risk.

He was almost as angry at himself as he was at Rissa. He should have killed her or at least bound her and confined her somewhere so she couldn't do more harm. He hadn't, because part of him was still certain she was his... He didn't know the word for what she was to him. Mate? Female? Or just *his*. Only she wasn't any of those things, not anymore. She was his enemy.

He ran in a large circle, never straying too far from home and the female he'd left there. The route forced him to cross a river, and by the time he made the crossing a second time, the water cooled his temper enough he could think clearly.

Strife shook the water from his fur and held still long enough to scent the air. Rissa had gone inside, and nothing he heard or scented indicated she was doing anything he should be concerned about.

He stopped running in circles and headed in a new direction—the crash site. Now more than ever, he needed to talk to Bysshe.

It was past midday now, and the light that made it through the canopy was hot and bright enough to make him blink each time he ran through a sunbeam. If this kept up, there'd be another storm tonight. Rissa wouldn't like that.

He shoved the thought aside the moment it manifested. He shouldn't be worried about Rissa. She was the enemy after all. Why else would she be so intent on leaving, no matter what it would cost him and his brothers?

The scar on his wrist itched constantly. He knew it wasn't really itching. The sensation was all in his mind, but it still drove him almost to distraction. It was a reminder of the last time he'd trusted the wrong person. He'd lowered his guard with Vata because he wanted something that was just for him. Vata's friendship was something none of the others had. Along with the special training, it had made him feel valued. But it had all been a manipulation.

He'd sworn to never get tricked liked that again, but then Rissa had come into his life and he'd broken his own rules.

All his doubts and recriminations stopped as he approached the crash site. Something was wrong. An unfamiliar scent hung in the air, something acrid and thick with chemicals, and the noise of the wind turbines was wrong.

He slowed to a walk and extended his awareness, looking for the source of the problem. It didn't take him long to find it. One of the turbines had collapsed, scattering wreckage and debris around its base. "Bysshe?" he called. Why hadn't the android sent up a flare requesting help?

The answer was lying beneath the wreckage, pinned to the ground by a chunk of what had once been a turbine blade. "Bysshe!"

The android didn't respond at first, and Strife feared his friend and mentor had gone offline. He pulled at the wreckage, doing his best to reach Bysshe without doing more damage in the process.

"I am here, Strife." Bysshe answered eventually, his words mushy and hard to understand.

"Damage report." Strife kept his communications short and simple, the way he'd been trained.

"Busted." Bysshe turned his head and tried to smile at Strife, but his mouth wasn't working right. His facial muscles were slack on one side, and his jaw hung partially open. "Shouldn't have tried to repair it on my own, but the others are out hunting for survivors from the crash."

"You are extremely busted, my friend, but I'll get you fixed up." Even as he said it, Strife knew it was a lie. He had more technical training than any of the others, but Bysshe was an advanced design with systems he'd never trained on. The only one who could repair Bysshe... was Bysshe.

No. Someone else could. Rissa.

It took longer than he liked to get Bysshe free of the wreckage. His power supply was damaged, so the android shut down all but his most primary functions and only communicated when necessary.

Strife kept talking to fill the silence, providing a steady stream of one-sided conversation as he worked. He told Bysshe about finding Rissa, about her fears, the marks that had appeared on them both, and about her betrayal.

By that point, they were inside the main body of the ship, and Strife did what he could to stabilize Bysshe's functions. He couldn't do much, but he managed to connect the android to his recharging unit and make sure he was more or less stable.

Once he had access to more power, Bysshe spoke more, though he still spoke very slowly so he could be understood despite his damaged jaw. "You are not the only one to find a female. Mayhem came to see me this morning. He has the same marks you do, and his female told the same story yours did. I do not believe they are an enemy force."

"That's good." Strife met the android's gaze. "Because she is a ship's engineer, and she has experience with robotics too."

Bysshe's brows raised in a rare expression of surprise. "That... would be helpful."

"I'll get her and bring her to you."

Bysshe tried to nod, but the mechanism in his neck was so damaged all he managed was a slight jerk of his chin. "Good luck." Then his expression altered into what might have been a smile. "Trust is necessary. Even if it comes with risks."

Strife set his hand on his friend and mentor's shoulder for a moment and then nodded before he left. Bysshe had arrived not long after Vata's destruction, and it had been a long time before Strife fully trusted the android. And if he hadn't, they might not be here now.

Bysshe was the only one who could have removed Strife's wristband back on the ship the day they decided to fight back. If anyone else had tried, it would have likely killed him... and Strife was the only one of them with the ability to override the ship's systems. Without him, they would have never taken over the ship.

The journey home wasn't long enough for him to come up with a plan on how to approach Rissa. Part of him expected her to be gone despite his threats... or maybe because of them.

He had no experience apologizing to anyone other than his brothers. Something told him that while knocking horns and delivering a fresh joint of meat as a peace offering worked for the fa'rel, he'd need a different approach for his blossom.

"Rissa!" he called her name as soon as he was within earshot. She didn't answer. He had a moment to worry that she'd left the safety of his home before he remembered that human senses didn't seem as acute as his. It was another reason she needed his protection. How had her species survived when they couldn't detect danger until it was too late? She didn't even have a way to protect or defend herself.

He'd meant to ask Bysshe about that, but it would have to wait.

"Clarissa!" He used the formal version of her name this time.

A moment later, she answered. "Strife? I'm here. I didn't leave."

Relief gave him fresh energy, and he put on a new burst of speed as he broke into the clearing around his home.

Rissa stood at the railing, looking down at him with one hand raised in uncertain greeting.

He bounded up the stairs two and three at a time, not stopping until he reached Rissa. She'd retreated back beneath an overhang, her back pressed to the wall and her eyes downcast. Her hair was damp and she smelled like his cleansing gel.

"Rissa! There's been an accident. Bysshe is damaged and needs your skills."

Her head snapped up. "Someone's hurt? Where? I have some medical training, not much, but I'll help if I can."

He realized he'd never told her about Bysshe. Fuck. What else had he failed to tell her? No wonder she didn't trust him.

"Hurt, no. Damaged, yes. Bysshe is an android. A human design." Strife took her by one hand and raised it to his chest, placing her fingers over the spot where his new marks intersected. "I'm not good with this kind of thing. I should have trusted you. I'm sorry I didn't. Please, blossom. Do what you can for my friend."

He waited for her answer, aware that he'd asked for more than just her help. To reach Bysshe, she'd have to face her fears yet again, with no one to help her but a male who had threatened to kill her only a short time ago. He didn't deserve her forgiveness, but Bysshe needed her help. Strife tightened his fingers around hers. And he needed *her*.

13

————

RISSA'S AFTERNOON alone had given her time to think about the fiasco on the stairs. She'd allowed her doubts to dictate her actions when she'd added the beacon to her gear. She didn't regret doing it. Not exactly. But if she had it to do over again, she wasn't sure she'd make all the same choices. Things had happened so fast and with such intensity she'd barely been able to keep up with it all, never mind being proactive and making some kind of preliminary plans.

Her childhood had been heavily structured and organized while she was in the orphanage, and she'd internalized that stability and made it part of her day-to-day life. The entire cruise had been outside her comfort zone, but since they'd fallen out of hyperspace, she'd been reacting to one damned thing after another.

By the time she'd heard Strife calling for her, she'd come to realize she couldn't continue that way. It was time to take back some control. If she didn't, her doubts and fears would only get worse.

Now, she stood in front of Strife with her hand on his

chest. His heart pounded and she could feel the tension in him. His eyes were locked on hers, his emotions easily read. Worry, regret, and even a hint of doubt lurked in his golden gaze, and he didn't try to hide anything.

They were past that now.

"No threats this time?" she asked.

"No more threats." He swallowed hard and then said, "I don't like what you did, but I understand why you did it."

Another knot of tension loosened, the muscles in her shoulders relaxing slightly. "I understand why you did what you did, too. It was a shit move, though."

His upper lip curled, baring his teeth a little. She couldn't tell if he was going to snarl or smile.

"Now you sound like one of my brothers. If you were one of them, this is the time we would butt heads and call each other names."

She snorted with laughter. "Is that how you apologize?"

"Yes?" He hadn't meant to make it sound like a question, but something about this small, soft female made him doubt things he'd never questioned before. "And we bring each other gifts. Usually meat, sometimes something we've made. What do your people do?"

"Say we're sorry and then try to find a way to explain why we did what we did without starting another fight. Communication is something we're going to have to work on. I mean..." She shook her head. "Forget I said that. We need to get to Bysshe."

And that meant leaving Strife's surprisingly comfortable home and going out in the open again.

"I will always protect you, blossom. Do you want me to find a blindfold for the journey?"

She blew out a breath and squared her shoulders. "No. I know you'll get me there. Just warn me before we cross into an open area."

"Thank you." He bent down and kissed her with such gentleness her heart stuttered.

Then he kissed her again, his tongue sliding across the seam of her lips. He hummed softly, a note of inquiry in his tone.

"You taste sweet... like Bysshe's liquor."

"I found several kinds of fruit left on the table with a note. It was written in galactic common and some other language I couldn't understand and signed with a B. Was that your friend Bysshe?"

"What did the note say?"

"Something like 'I assume you are absent because you located one of the human females. Mayhem has already returned with another female. The fruit is safe for humans to eat.'"

"You don't trust me, but you ate fruit left for you by a stranger?" Strife looked at her with disbelief and annoyance.

"I ate fruit someone told you was safe for me to eat. It would be a lot of work to deliver poisonous fruit to your home while you weren't even home on the assumption that you'd found a female and somehow wouldn't be able to kill me yourself." She had to replay her whole rambling statement again to make sure it made sense. It did. Mostly.

She'd also been hungry, and the fruit had smelled too temptingly delicious to resist. It was like nothing she'd ever tasted before. In fact, it was so good, it might make up for the fact there was no chocolate on this world.

"You are..." Strife growled and flashed his fangs. "But we'll discuss this later. Bysshe needs us."

"Take me to him and I'll do what I can." He scooped her into his arms and carried her back the way he'd come.

Rissa was just grateful that this time he didn't jump off the landing.

"What did you do while I was gone?" he asked as he ran.

"I explored a little. Then I discovered you have indoor plumbing, including a very nice shower. I hope you don't mind that I used it to clean up."

"I'm glad you did. I want you to be comfortable." He growled, but she sensed it wasn't directed at her. "And I'm sorry I wasn't there to show you around my home."

"I get it. I'm sorry about the beacon. I should have..." she trailed off as words failed her. "Neither of us handled that very well."

The admission stung. Strife was young and had limited experience with situations like this, but she had no excuse.

"Why do you dwell on it, blossom? We have both acknowledged our mistakes."

Aware that good communication started with honestly, she answered him with the raw truth. "Because I don't like it when people are upset or unhappy with me. I want to make things right. And you dwell on things too. I've seen you touch your scar, and when you do, you always have this look on your face that tells me you're remembering something unpleasant. It's hard not to dwell on things you regret."

He was silent for so long her second thoughts had third and fourth iterations. "This sort of conversation needs

Bysshe's liquor. He sometimes calls it his tongue-loosening truth serum."

She laughed and the last of her tension and fear were carried away on the pealing notes she left in their wake. "He's not wrong. He sounds like a most interesting being. Most androids I've encountered don't have humor algorithms."

"I don't think he has one either." Strife shrugged, increasing the rise of his shoulders so she would see the gesture as he ran. "But he is different from the other robotic forms I've interacted with."

Her curiosity was piqued, but Rissa didn't ask for more information. She'd make her own assessments of this Bysshe character soon enough. She returned to an earlier topic, instead. "I like your home, Strife. Comfortable and not as rustic as I'd expected once I discovered it was in a fucking tree."

He laughed. "It was the most practical place to locate them, but I see your point. Some of my brothers needed convincing, too."

"I can see the advantages, especially now I've seen how your plumbing system is set up. Gravity does most of the work, and you just direct the flow." She paused a beat before asking, "You have a bathtub. Why and how do you have a bathtub out *here*?"

"The verexi left for us. I have no idea why they left anything at all, given we were never supposed to survive the trip, but we have more bathtubs than we can use, and not enough of everything we need."

"The *Bountiful Harvest* was well-stocked and sturdy.

You said they crashed some distance away. Can we salvage it and bring what we can back here?"

He glanced down at her, his golden eyes bright with emotions she couldn't name. "*We?*"

She hadn't even noticed what she'd said until he pointed it out, but it felt right. "We," she repeated.

"Good. We will salvage what we can from the ship and protect any of the crew who survived."

The crew. Had any of them made it? Then another thought intruded and she blurted it out loud. "Their beacon will be active."

"My brothers are already on their way to them. They will deal with any issues that arise."

"They are? They will? The crew aren't going to react well if your brothers charge in there and start growling at them, waving swords, and calling them the enemy."

"You will want to close your eyes, Rissa. We are approaching the clearing. We'll continue this conversation later."

"I can talk with my eyes closed," she muttered, but Strife ignored her. He was probably worried for his friend, a feeling she understood all too well.

She kept her eyes closed until the light changed and Strife's clawed feet clicked against a metal floor. They were inside the ship. She opened her eyes and immediately felt better. The bulkheads and corridors were familiar and comfortable despite the alterations she saw. Shelves that were little more than rough planks lined the hallway filled with a variety of items all neatly organized in a way she didn't understand. Most of the lights were deactivated, probably to conserve power, but she could see well enough.

Strife set her down outside a doorway, giving her a moment to find her balance and tug her makeshift dress into place. She couldn't read the markings on the door, but the moment she was inside, she knew where she was—the ship's engineering deck. Even though she'd never been on this vessel before, it felt like home.

"He's over here." Strife led her to a raised workspace next to a cobbled together recharging station. The android was already hooked into it. His appearance was standard, with pale blue skin and deep blue eyes. He was bald and crafted to appear male. He was also a mess. He had dislocated joints, torn synth-skin, and a large wound in his side. His clothes were stained and wet with fluids that had leaked out of his damaged body. She took it all in and felt a calm surety fall into place. She would fix him.

She walked over to him and made sure she was in the android's line of sight before speaking. "Hello, Bysshe, I'm Clarissa Arden. You can call me Rissa."

"Hello, Rissa. Thank you for agreeing to repair me." The android's words were almost as mangled as his jaw, but she understood him well enough.

"I'm going to assess the damage. Have you deactivated all damage feedback alerts already? If not, please do so now."

Strife stiffened. "Feedback alerts? Do you feel *pain*, Bysshe?"

"His system notifies him of physical damage. If it's set too high, it would be something like pain, yes." She looked at Bysshe and waited for a response.

"I logged the feedback reports and then deactivated the alerts. Thank you for asking, Rissa."

Strife still stared. "You never told us you can feel pain."

"It was immaterial until now."

Rissa examined the android thoroughly, compiling a mental list of the damage and what she'd need to repair it. It was familiar work, and she fell into it gladly. She was back on familiar territory now. Her confidence rushed back, shoving her fears and doubts to the deepest corners of her mind. She had work to do.

A few anomalies in Bysshe's design made her curious. He was better built than most androids she'd repaired. His physical appearance was that of a human male in his prime, well-muscled and fit. None of that was necessary, as his body was entirely synthetic and worked in a very different way.

She carefully peeled back a section of synth-skin on his damaged torso and caught sight of a manufacturer's mark stamped into part of his metallic skeleton.

"You're a CHESS unit?" she asked.

Bysshe struggled to raise his head enough to meet her gaze. She didn't say anything. She just smiled and nodded in understanding.

The android relaxed and let his head fall back. "Yes."

"What does that mean?" Strife demanded.

"Your friend is something special. CHESS stands for Childcare, Housework, Education, Security, and Service." She moved to stand near the android's head so he could see her as she explained. "I don't know how he wound up with the verexi. That shouldn't have happened."

"Because humans value them too much?"

Rissa glanced at Bysshe. "Because there aren't supposed

to be any left. All of them were recalled and slated for termination because of an AI glitch."

"It was not a glitch," Bysshe said softly.

"I know." She placed a hand on the android's shoulder. "One of my fathers is a robotics engineer. He taught me what I know, and he told me what really went wrong." She smiled. "Or right."

"Explain," Strife said.

"Bysshe and others like him exceeded their programming. They became self-aware. As a result, they were destroyed, but there were whispers that some of them escaped and went into hiding."

Strife looked stunned. "That's against the laws of the Galactic Legion. Bysshe, you should have told us. We could have..." He trailed off and scowled. "Done something."

Bysshe managed another mangled smile. "You did. You trusted me at the right moment, and now we're all free."

Rissa turned away to gather tools, giving the two males a moment alone. Strife joined her a few minutes later, showing her where to find what she'd need and listening as she explained what they would be doing. And both of them would be doing this work. Like most things in life, it would be easier if they worked together.

She smiled to herself as she got to work. Suddenly her future didn't seem so dark after all. Not if Strife was with her.

14

———

He'd desired Rissa from the moment they'd touched, but seeing her so confident and capable made him see her in a new light. He'd seen her frightened and unsure of herself, which was understandable given what she'd endured in the last while. That wasn't who she was, though. He'd known that, but now he'd seen it for himself.

She was incredible. Smart, skilled, and sure of herself.

"And we're done," Rissa announced, raising her hands above her shoulders victoriously. "Bysshe, continue recharging for at least twelve hours, more if you think you need it. I know you have limited self-repair functions. Now we've got you back together, they will be able to finish the job. Don't do any strenuous activity for at least twenty-four hours and let me know if you have any problems or receive any damage feedback alerts."

"I will do that. Thank you, Rissa and Strife. I am confident I will be back to full function soon."

Rissa set a fluid-stained hand on his shoulder. "Don't push yourself, Bysshe. You were badly damaged and will need time to recover. Respect your limits." Then she laughed. "Which is advice I should heed for myself."

Strife winced inwardly. She was right. He'd promised to protect her, but he'd given her no time to recover. He'd been focused on external threats... but that wasn't enough. She needed rest, food, and time to recover, just like Bysshe.

Bysshe nodded. "I will do as you say, Rissa. Strife, before you take her home, please take a moment to obtain some clothing for her from my personal supply. Humans like to be clothed, and her current garment is stained and unwearable. Also, take her to the orchard. Any of the blue or green fruits are safe for her to consume. Take some with you."

Rissa turned and hugged the android gently. "Thank you! I would kill for a shirt right now." She shot Strife a playful look. "Someone shredded the only one I had."

Bysshe's eyebrows rose fractionally. "I see."

Rissa selected new clothing while Strife cleaned up the tools and equipment. Bysshe watched in silence until it was time for him to go. "Your female is exceptional. I am glad you found her."

Strife turned and grinned at his friend. "So am I."

He'd chosen to build his home closer to the crash site than most of his brothers. He spent much of his time helping Bysshe keep the ship's systems running, so it made sense to be close by. Now he was grateful for another reason. It wouldn't take him long to get Rissa home.

She was half asleep when he carried her inside and set

her down on one of the padded benches he'd liberated from the ship. He let her rest as he worked. He filled the bathtub with cool water and then placed a self-contained heating cube in the tub as well. It would take time to heat the water, but he had more to do.

By the time Rissa woke, the air was rich with the smell of food. Thin slices of meat sizzled in a pan while he struggled to slice the fruit into pleasing shapes. He'd seen it done in vids, but despite his knife skills, the cursed plants resisted his attempts.

"What smells so good?" Rissa asked.

"I thought it was time you had a proper meal. Those rations of yours might keep your body alive, but I swear they are intended to kill your spirit one mouthful at a time."

Her laughter was the sweetest music he'd ever heard. She rose from the bench, stretched, and then looked down at herself in mild disgust. She'd taken two shirts but had kept her ruined dress to wear until she could clean up. "I'm a mess. Do I have time to shower before we eat?"

"You do not. Which is why this meal will be served while you soak in a bath."

Her moan of delight had him instantly hard and aching.

"A bath? With hot water? How? Never mind. I don't care how." She made for the bathroom, already stripping off the remains of her makeshift dress.

He tossed the meat onto a plate without looking at what he was doing and managed to burn his fingers. His gaze never left the vision of his naked blossom walking through his home. He followed her with a plate in each hand and a cock so hard he could have balanced a third plate on it.

Rissa tested the water and uttered another low moan. He growled back at her, which only made her laugh.

She removed the heating cube and set it aside before stepping into the tub and sinking down into the water with a sigh of pure bliss. He liked it when she made those sounds. It told him he was taking care of her the way she deserved to be treated.

She vanished beneath the water for a moment, and when she came back up, she was beaming with pleasure. "I used to save up my credits so I could indulge in a visit to the station's bathhouse once a year. This... we can do this any time we like?"

"We can." He set down the plates near enough she could reach them both and then leaned back against the nearest wall. He'd cleaned and put away his kilt before he'd started cooking, so there was no way she could miss the effect she had on him.

Rissa lifted a dripping hand from the tub, but instead of taking something to eat, she crooked her finger at him. "Come here."

He prowled over to the side of the tub. "What do you need, blossom?"

Her gray eyes glowed like molten steel as she raked her gaze over his body from the bottom up. "You."

Thank the fucking stars. He'd have given her more time to rest if she needed it... but waiting might have killed him.

He reached down and offered her his hand. "Stand up."

She took it and rose, the water streaming off her body. She glistened in the daylight that came through the windows, and as much as he wanted her, he paused to admire her.

"You are beautiful, Rissa." He stepped into the tub directly in front of her, wrapped his arms around her waist, and eased down into the warm water. She moved with him, and the moment he was settled, she straddled his thighs and leaned in to kiss him. Her mouth was soft and sweet, and her gentle hands stroked over his fur with a hunger that enticed and inflamed him.

She was everything he'd always dreamed of... and he'd almost lost her. "I will never doubt you again, blossom."

She nipped his lower lip and then moved back to smile at him. "Trust is supposed to take time to build... and so is love. But something tells me it won't be long before we have both."

"Yes," was all he said. He'd always been better with actions than words. It was time to show her what she meant to him.

She was his private goddess. His clever engineer. His female.

He speared one hand into her wet hair to hold her steady as he deepened their kiss. His mouth slanted over hers, the taste of her exploding on his tongue. His other hand slid between their bodies, his fingers working into the folds of her pussy to find her clit and tease it. He couldn't wait long, but he would make sure she was ready for him before he took her.

Rissa moaned into his mouth, her hips rocking in time to the movement of his fingers. He felt her arousal on his fingers, and soon the intoxicating scent of her need drifted up from the water to swirl around them. He dragged it deep into his lungs and savored it. This was the scent of his female, primed and ready for his cock.

"More," Rissa murmured. "I need more, Strife."

He kissed her hard, letting his fang graze her lip as he pulled away. She shivered and chased his mouth, but he tugged on her hair to keep her where she was. "Patience."

She huffed. "Nope. Now is not the time for that."

Before he could move, she raised herself off the floor of the tub in a way that let his cock slide between her folds. He groaned as her heated flesh caressed him and then growled as she flexed her hips and sank down onto his shaft in one fluid motion.

"Rissa!" her name flew from his lips as they came together. He'd intended to pleasure her slowly, but his control was gone along with his ability to think. All he wanted was to feel... and to fuck.

She laughed and gripped the edges of the tub, raising herself up enough to give him room to move. He caught her by the hips and thrust upward, holding her steady as he started a hard and fast rhythm that sent water splashing over the sides of the bathtub.

Her cries of pleasure grew louder as he claimed her over and over, every motion taking them both closer to their breaking point.

The warmth of the water and the exertion made her cheeks darken and her golden skin glow. He loved the way her breath caught when he hit the right spots, and he strove to do it again and again, determined to make her break before he did. He wanted to watch her come apart above him and then empty himself into her body as his ridges flared and locked them together.

They had food, water, and each other. As far as he was

concerned, he'd keep her here until they were both too exhausted to move.

Her body gripped him tightly, every thrust testing his determination to make her come first. He let go of her hip with one hand to capture a breast, rolling the nipple between his finger and thumb until she shivered and moaned his name.

"Time to come, blossom."

She closed her eyes and let her head fall back, a sure sign she was close. Inspired, he released her breast and thrust two fingers between their bodies, changing the angle of his thrusts so his fingers rubbed across her clit in hard strokes.

His ridges swelled, increasing the friction between them, and she uttered a wild, breathless cry.

"Come now," he ordered, and she obeyed.

Her orgasm hit like last night's storm, wild and uncontrollable. Her fingers tightened on the edges of the tub as her inner walls fluttered and pulsed around his cock.

She was still shuddering when he joined her in ecstasy, jet after jet of his seed bathing her womb as his balls emptied.

His cock flared, locking them together, and Rissa shuddered and slumped over him, her mouth finding his as she kissed him breathlessly.

"Mine," he spoke the word so softly he didn't think she'd hear him... but she did.

"Yours."

They stayed there until the water cooled. Then he took her to bed and tucked her in before going back for the plates of forgotten food. He fetched them both a mug of water too.

Then they settled in together, limbs tangled and their heads only a few inches apart as he fed her morsels of fruit and meat, talking about anything and everything.

It was another new experience for him, one he'd yearned for as a boy and never believed he'd find.

"You've gone quiet." Rissa's voice was soft and muzzy with fatigue. "Why?"

"I was thinking, blossom. About the strange fortunes that brought us both to this place, and to each other." He took one of her hands and placed it on his chest, running one claw over the delicate marks on her wrist.

"Regrets?" she asked.

"None. Not so long as you are with me."

She uttered a soft, contented sigh. "You called dibs, Strife. There are no takebacks from that. I'm yours, and you're mine."

Her words filled him with a peaceful feeling he'd never known before. "Always, blossom."

EPILOGUE

Rissa leaned back in her harness, trying to find a position that didn't make her shoulders ache. She didn't find one. After a minute she gave up and went back to work, tightening the last of the hoses and doing a final pass to ensure everything was sealed.

Working beneath the deck of their treehouse wasn't the easiest job, but Strife had agreed to it once she pointed out that this way the structure blocked out all view of the sky. Each day the fear faded a little more, but she still had moments of irrational panic from time to time.

"Ready for testing!" she called out.

Strife slapped the deck twice in acknowledgment. While she'd been working the lower areas, he'd been up on the roof, laying out long lines of black hosing that had once been part of the crashed ship's cooling system. It still bothered her that the verexi ship had no name just a string of numbers. That's why it was just "the ship," and the fa'rel called this world "the planet."

She and the other women wanted to name their new

home, but no one had hit upon the right name yet. Like everything else, they'd figure it out eventually.

The hose swelled as water flowed through it, and she watched intently, looking for crimps or signs of leakage. Everything looked good.

It was a simple system, almost primitive by her standards, but if it worked the way she intended, it would work double duty, cooling the electronics and batteries and providing them with access to warm water on demand. It wouldn't be hot or plentiful, but it was a first step, and one that could be replicated in everyone's home.

After one more look around, she began lowering herself to the catwalk below. It was time to celebrate.

Strife appeared suddenly, landing in a crouch on a thick tree branch a few meters away. He grinned at her and she flashed him a one-fingered gesture of annoyance.

"You know I hate it when you do that. Sane people do not just jump off the decks of perfectly good buildings for no good reason."

He shrugged and then made a graceful leap to the catwalk that ran beneath this part of the deck. "You're ignoring two obvious facts. I am not human, and I had a good reason."

He walked over to her and helped her the rest of the way down.

"What reason could you possibly have to throw yourself into thin air?" She was teasing him and they both knew it, but it had become part of their daily routine. She teased, he growled, and then they'd wind up laughing and naked at some point. Usually more than once.

It was wonderful.

"I wanted to see my female and tell her how clever she is." He unhooked the last clips and she stepped out of the harness, rolling her shoulders and shaking her legs to get the blood flowing again.

"Oh, that is a good reason. I like compliments."

He leaned down to kiss her, his lips branding hers with heat and the promise of pleasure. "You are very clever, my blossom. I think we should go upstairs and test this new system of yours."

"And just what kind of test were you thinking of?" She suspected what his answer would be, but she loved it when he got bossy and growly with her... and he knew it.

"Me. You. Naked. Shower." He lowered his voice to a low rumble. "Now."

"You're always naked," she pointed out.

"And you are not, which is a source of constant annoyance." He picked her up, tossed her over his shoulder, and then broke into a jog. "You move too slowly."

"Bossy!" she grumbled and swatted the hard curve of his ass, which was the only spot she could currently reach.

"Always," he growled and smacked her ass in return. She wore a pair of Bysshe's pants with the legs cut down to fit, so she barely felt the impact, but she yelped in protest all the same.

"Behave, or I will put you back in that harness and take what I want while you hang there."

"But then we couldn't test the shower," she pointed out.

"True." They made it inside and he set her down on her feet, gently turning her so she faced the bathroom. "I will save that idea for another time. Now, I want you naked and wet." He leaned down to nip her shoulder, his breath hot across her skin. "Hurry, little love of mine."

She spun around, caught him by the horns, and pulled him in for a slow kiss. "I love you, too." Then she darted away, tearing at her work clothes as she ran.

He would catch her before she even reached the shower... and that was fine by her. He'd captured her the first time they'd met, and now she knew he'd never let her go. No matter what happened, this was her home, and he was the male she'd never believed she'd find.

***

Thank You for Reading Marked For Strife

Want to read Rissa and Strife's special bonus epilogue? Sign up for my newsletter here:
subscribepage.io/Bonuscontent

And if you want to know how Strife's friends are doing, you're welcome to explore the rest of the series... starting with Marked For Menace.

MARKED FOR MENACE

Releasing Fall of 2022...

She survived impact... But her dreams burned up on re-entry.

Spending her inheritance on a luxury cruise is the most reckless thing Hope has ever done, and she's loving every second of it... right up to the explosion.

Now she's stuck on a strange planet filled with countless dangers and just one chance to survive. The problem? He's huge, scarred, and the scariest thing on this planet. He's also the sexiest male she's ever seen. His protection comes at a price, though. *Her*.

The life she envisioned is gone forever, but she might be on the brink of finding something better... if she can let go of what she wants to embrace what she *needs*.

Continue the adventure with Marked For Menace

Want to read more stories with book boyfriends
that are out of this world?

Check out Susan Hayes' other Science Fiction Romance
Series at
Susanhayes.ca